KILDARE

CARLOW

WEXFORD

BLACKSTAIRS MOUNTAINS

IRELAND

THE START OF THE JOURNEY

GLENCOPPALEEN

C000176719

In the darkness of the night the unicorns float
like pearly ghosts, landing as softly as snowflakes to
feed on the shimmering moon-daisies.

Suddenly they begin to droop like fading flowers,
and the Company of the Hare — Aunt Emm,
Jennifer and the Major — spring into action . . .

The last unicorns of the western world are being led
from the hidden valley of Glencoppaleen to the
mysterious island of Inishnallis, 'sometimes there and
sometimes not', where they will be safe.

The Company has powerful allies on its long journey.
The Weaver of the Winds provides a flying-horse
compass and a magic flute, and sends them guides
— an owl by night, a starling by day; Nutmouse dons
many hats to foil the Enemy; and Gertrude Speede
lives up to her name when all seems lost.

But evil forces are arrayed against them, intent on
destroying the herd for the sake of their twisted golden
horns. The sinister Mr. Potts, his cohorts Evil
and Chop, and his malignant army of rooks and
crows dog their footsteps along the way.

The fortunes of war sway to and fro. There are
triumphs and tragedies, and a final deadly encounter in
the Wood of the Yew.

Inishnallis beckons, but can
they overcome the last obstacle
and reach it before it disappears . . . ?

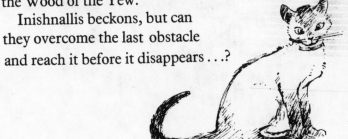

Shelagh Jones

SAVE the UNICORNS

Illustrated by Terry Myler

THE CHILDREN'S PRESS

To Joan

First published 1989 by
The Children's Press
45 Palmerston Road, Dublin 6

© Text Shelagh Jones
© Illustrations The Children's Press

ISBN 0 947962 48 4 paperboards
ISBN 0 947962 50 6 paper

Typeset by Computertype Limited
Printed by Mount Salus Press, Dublin

Contents

1. The Box on the Corner

*In which Jennifer is sent to post a letter
in a box that should not be there; Trip trips the
chemist; and Squiff is released.*

The newspaper rustled, indicating my Aunt Emm's
disapproval. I helped myself to another piece of toast, spread
it thickly with butter and Aunt Emm's apple and orange jelly-
marmalade, and re-read Mum's letter:

I do hope you are having a good time at Aunt Emmeline's.
She's a funny old thing, I know, but her heart is in the
right place and she does enjoy having a young person to
stay. Dad and I will be home in three weeks' time, so it
will not be long before we see you. Dad's business is going
very well, and I truly believe that my being here has
helped.

'Liar!' I thought. 'You just wanted a trip to Paris.' I folded
the letter and replaced it in the envelope (I am a naturally
tidy person, Mum says) and looked towards my aunt.

'Her heart is in the right place.' There was not much of
Aunt Emm showing except her long fingers, knobbly with
old age and great carbuncle rings, and whitened at the
moment by the manner in which she was gripping the
newspaper.

The newspaper rustled again. Whatever my aunt was
reading, it did *not* meet with her approval.

'May I have another piece of toast?' I asked.

The newspaper lowered, revealing my aunt's high-
cheekboned face, her pinched, slightly-hooked nose, mild blue

7

eyes and the almost unlined forehead, framed by a frizz of hair which had not turned grey but had remained a surprising honey-blonde.

'Of course you may,' she said. 'Make it yourself.'

I left the table and passed through the baize-covered swing door that separated the kitchen from the dining-room. In this old, three-storied terrace house where my aunt chose to live there were few what my mother called 'modern applicances'. Toast was not made in an electric toaster, but between the heated ring and heavy lid of an ancient Aga cooker. I cut two thick slices of brown bread (my aunt disliked paper-wrapped pre-sliced loaves, preferring to bake her own), slipped them on to the broad slate-grey circle and gently lowered the top. I was aware that my every move was being watched by Tripitaka, curled on one corner of the stove, dark-chocolate paws tucked underneath him. That is to say I *think* I was being watched; you never can tell with a cat that squints.

'Tripitaka?' I had asked when we were introduced. 'Trip-i-TAH-ka!' (holding on to the middle 'a' in the manner of my aunt, so that the sound echoed round the stone-floored kitchen). 'What a funny name for a cat.'

'It's a very good name,' my aunt had said crisply. 'An Eastern name for an Eastern cat. Surely you've heard of the monk Tripitaka, who brought the stories of the Buddha to China, and of his friend Monkey? Don't they teach you *anything* at school?'

'Of course they do,' I said defensively. 'We're going to learn how to use computers next term.'

My aunt gave what can only be described as a snort. 'Feeding in a lot of rubbish supplied by other people. They should be teaching you how to THINK.'

I decided to drop the subject. 'Well, I shall call him "Trip",' I had said decidedly, putting out my hand to stroke the cat's cream and chocolate fur. '*That* is a good name for a cat; they're always underfoot.'

Tripitaka had looked beyond me with indifference. 'Call me what you like,' he seemed to say. 'Any name is the same to me. But do not accuse me of being "underfoot". This is *my* kitchen.' I had drawn my hand away. Suitably scolded.

Breakfast was finished in silence. We cleared away and washed up in silence, too. The article my aunt had been reading must have upset her greatly, for the silence was punctuated by her sighs. I glanced at the newspaper as I took the cloth from the table but found little there that might have caused her distress.

'PLANT TO CLOSE—More Jobs Lost' was the top headline, followed by 'CRIME RATE RISES'. There were details of an argument between two politicians and of a new development in Anglo-Irish relations—neither of interest as my aunt always stated that she passed politics by. There were only two other stories: 'Increase in Petrol Prices'—but she hardly ever used her small battered car; and a short piece in the right-hand corner headed 'Hydro-electric Power Plan Gets Go-Ahead'. That was all.

Shrugging my shoulders, I went upstairs to make my bed. I lingered, reading a page of my book between each section of the operation; one page puff the pillow, another page smooth out the sheet, third page pull up the blankets, fourth page put on the eiderdown. At home the job took next to no time, for I had a duvet; here, there were sheets, blankets, bedcover, eiderdown. All to be straightened and tucked in.

When I came down again, my aunt was dusting the ornaments in the china-cupboard. She was still sighing. Obviously, there was to be no outing today. No walk along the Canal to find the weird little creatures tucked into the grass beside the water; no trip to the Green to feed the ducks; no wandering round the Museum to examine the quaint objects of long-ago; no stopping at our favourite cafe to drink hot chocolate and eat sticky buns. People might consider it boring to go and stay with a great-aunt. But, with Aunt Emm, one was always seeing things that one had not dreamed were there before.

Today, however, was going to be different. I went outside, into the garden.

The garden was like a shadow of the house, as long and narrow as the house was tall and thin. It was not very tidy, for my aunt did not believe in trim gardening. She put plants she loved here, there, and everywhere, and they bloomed, profusely. Now, it was June and the roses out-flowered everything. Aunt Emm's roses came from all over the world and stretched back into history. Tiny pale-yellow roses from China romped up the garden wall, sending out whiffs of tea from their clustered petals; a white rose from the Himalayas rampaged through the apple tree; the pink-and-white rose, *Félicité et Pérpetue* (raised, my aunt said, in France and named for two saints), mounted in prim neatly-packed flowers, tier upon tier towards the heavens. Damask roses brought from the east by the Crusaders shared a bed with fat cabbage roses, like those in old Dutch paintings, and Bonnie Prince Charlie's *Jacobite* glowed pale ivory in a dark corner. There were pink roses like spun silk, and dark crimson ones, richly scented, with petals like velvet, which my aunt distilled into rose-water or dried for pot-pourri.

Against the brick wall at the end of the garden, close to a clump of lavender, was a row of hives for bees. 'Fancy keeping bees in a crowded city!' I had said.

'Why not?' my aunt had demanded. 'There is plenty of food for them here,' (indicating the pale flowers of thyme, weighed down with buzzing, busy bodies). 'And there are lime trees along the Canal—lime-honey is delicious.' Later in the summer, she told me, she would pack the hives into the back of her ramshackle old car, and take the bees for their holiday on the hills. 'To drink the heather,' she explained.

Picking my way across the daisied lawn, I sat upon the swing which hung from a large old pear tree, halfway down the garden. If one swung high enough, one could see into next door.

This was a very different sort of garden from my aunt's. Leggy unhealthy-looking vegetables and strange ugly herbs I could not name stood in straight rows upon the beaten earth. A stump of a tree without any branches made a brave effort to send forth a few spindly shoots with sad-looking leaves. Much of the space was taken up by concrete outhouses. Somehow these looked sinister, for they had no windows. Mr. Potts, who owned the house, always kept them locked.

Mr. Potts did not like one looking into his garden. I discovered this on the day of my arrival. Whenever he saw my head bob up above the wall, he would shout something and shake his fist. He did not like cats either. If Tripitaka appeared in his garden he would throw things at him.

Mr. Potts kept a chemist's shop in the city. Aunt Emm and I had passed it one day on one of our outings.

Eughan Potts
M.P.S.I: B.E.A: B.S.R: M.M.

was written above the door, in quaint old-fashioned script.

'What do all the letters mean?' I had asked my aunt.

'Mr. Potts is more than he would seem,' was the reply. My aunt had pressed her lips together in a disapproving manner. If Mr. Potts did not like girls or cats, it was clear that my aunt did not like Mr. Potts.

After lunch, my aunt broke her silence.

'I have written a letter,' she informed me. 'It is important that it catches the next post. Will you take it down to the box on the corner, please?'

'But—' Bewildered, I began to protest. I had been staying with Aunt Emm long enough to know that there was no post-box on the corner. Not at this end, nor at the other, where the road runs down to the Canal. The nearest box was at the sub-post-office, two streets away.

'Let there be no "but" about it. This letter is important. It is imperative that it goes *at once,* and from the corner-box.'

Aunt Emm pressed the letter into my hand. Her large handwriting was scrawled all over a pink envelope that smelled faintly of apple-blossom:

Major Fitzwilliam Harker, D.S.M.M: S.P: W.W.

('More letters!' I thought. 'Perhaps he, too, is more than he would seem.')

Honeydew Cottage,
Glencoppaleen,
Co. Wexford

'You may take Tripitaka with you,' my aunt was saying. 'He needs a walk.'

Now it was my turn to sigh! It is one thing to be asked to post a letter in a box that is not there. One can get round that, somehow. But the fact that one is dragging a cat about on a lead is something one cannot conceal. A dog would be all right; it might be rather fun, really. We have never had one; Mum does not like them. A cat on a lead is *not* fun. People stare.

There were no people to stare, however, as Tripitaka and I stepped through the front door and along the short path to the iron gate. The street was empty. One glance to my right confirmed what I knew in advance. There was *no* post-box on the corner. I looked to my left, to the other end of the street, where the Canal gleamed like a sheet of bluish metal set down to reflect the sky. I gasped!

As I have said, there were no people in the street. And there were no parked cars. My view was unimpeded. Yet there, solid and green, at the corner of the street, stood a post-box.

My first thought (rather a foolish one, really, for I would have seen the postal workers doing it) was that the box must have been erected recently. But, as I approached, with Tripitaka treading the pavement in a manner that suggested that the slabs were too rough and grimy for his precious paws, it became obvious that the box, though freshly painted, was very old indeed. It was smaller than the usual kind, octagonal in shape, and had a knob on the top that made it look as if it was wearing a tam-o-shanter hat. Embossed on the front were the letters V.R. and a crown, indicating that it dated from the reign of Queen Victoria. I looked at the little inset label to see what time the next collection would be. It was blank.

While I was considering whether it was wise to entrust my aunt's letter to so strange a box, a hand—a small brown hand, with chestnut hairs growing thickly on it—came out of the slot, and snatched the envelope from my grasp.

I was saved from the full shock and worry of this event by the sudden appearance of a Cairn terrier. He burst from the corner house and bounded to the gate, yapping viciously. Trip leapt several feet into the air, uttered an unpleasant Siamese yowl, and whisking the lead from my hand streaked round the corner to disappear along the road that runs by the Canal. I set off, in pursuit.

We covered three corners of the block at speed, and approached my aunt's house just as Mr. Potts was descending from his little van, balancing a large, flat cardboard box before him. Trip dodged between his feet, the lead wound round his ankles and, unable to see, Mr. Potts took a step forward, and fell crashing to the ground. The contents of the box were released, and began to run around the pavement in all directions.

'I'm terribly sorry.'

I stared, open-mouthed, at the scuttering guinea-pigs that were rapidly escaping along the gutter and under gates into people's front gardens. Tripitaka was sitting at my aunt's front gate, licking his paws.

'Help me!'

Crawling on his hands and knees, Mr. Potts was plucking guinea-pigs from the street and tossing them, very roughly I thought, back into the box. I bent and picked up the little animal that was sniffing at my toes.

'Don't give him back!' A hand gripped mine, and held it firmly. My aunt had come out of her house and was standing beside me. Mr. Potts turned a face that was white with wrath towards her. Crouching on the pavement, he looked like a malignant black and white toad.

'That cat is a menace,' he snarled. 'It ought to be destroyed.'

'Oh, I don't know.' My aunt's reply was mild. 'He has a way with mice.'

Following her up the path, I chuckled to myself. Tripitaka did, indeed, have 'a way with mice'. It was his own special

way. Each time he ventured into Mr. Potts's garden, he would return carrying a small mouse carefully in his mouth. He would lay the little creature at my aunt's feet, and she would release it into her garden, where it would live happily and unmolested.

When the front door had shut behind us, I took the guinea-pig from the safety of my pocket. He was quite a young one, small enough to sit in the palm of my hand. He gazed up at me with his bright-bead eyes. He was chequered; black and white and tan. The ruff of hair that framed his small round head was white one side of his face, tan the other. I stroked him gently with my finger.

'You are squew-wiff-squint,' I told him. And so he was named. Squew-wiff; Squiff, for short!

2. The Hidden Herd

In which a reply to the letter is received;
Jennifer and Aunt Emm take a trip into the country;
and the Major sounds a gloomy note.

I was in the back garden, helping my aunt with her bees, when the reply to her letter came.

'That will be the postman,' she said, suddenly.

I looked up, surprised. I had heard nothing.

'Well! Don't keep him waiting.' My aunt was impatient. 'Go to the front door and fetch the letter. You will find a jar of honey on the dresser, as you pass through the kitchen. Give him that.'

Taking off my hat and veil, I hurried to do as I was told. On my way through the kitchen I collected the jar of honey, and went into the long passageway that cut through the centre of the house and acted as the hall. As I stepped into the passage, I heard the sound that I supposed must have come within my aunt's earshot in the garden. A piercing whistle was shrilling through the house. Someone—the postman, presumably—was whistling through the letter-box on the front door.

'What an odd way to attract attention,' I thought. 'Why doesn't he ring the bell, or knock?' When I opened the door, the answer to my question was supplied at once. The little man standing on the doorstep could barely reach the letter-box.

At first, I though I was looking at a child. But the wrinkles round the tiny creature's bright black eyes proclaimed him to be quite old, and he had gingery whiskers protruding from

16

his jaw ('A bit like Squiff's,' I thought). 'My—my aunt said to give you this,' I stammered.

The little man grunted as he took the jar. The letter that he thrust into my hand was in a pale blue envelope. As I took it, I could not help noticing his hand. It was the same as the one that had snatched the letter from my grasp, three days before.

'Thank you,' I said. The little man made no reply. He grunted again, pulled his postman's cap further down over his nose, turned, and made off down the path. On reaching the gate, he did not open it, but gave a hop and a skip. He jumped clear over the top, and vanished. I rushed back to my aunt.

'Never mind the messenger. Just give me the message.' She cut short my garbled flow of words. Tearing open the envelope, she read the short note that it contained, and passed it to me.

Dear Emmeline:
Message received and understood. Suggest conference, and planned manoeuvre.

Ever Yours
Toby Fitzwilliam Harker

The letterhead bore a crest, I noticed. A tiny hare. Very like the talisman my aunt wore round her neck.

'I don't quite understand that.' I returned the letter to my aunt. 'What does it mean?'

'The meaning is quite plain.'

My aunt bent closer to the hives. 'Some friends of ours are in danger. They must be rescued,' she told the bees.

We set off next morning in my aunt's car, leaving Tripitaka to mind Squiff and the house. My aunt's car was very old and difficult to start, but once on our way and clear of the city traffic it bowled along at a fine pace. Aunt Emm drove with the window open, so that her hair was blown about and looked even more untidy than before. I sat beside her, clutching the road-map, which was not really needed as the roads were so clearly sign-posted. Behind us on the back seat was the picnic-basket.

We stopped for lunch at an old country churchyard, sitting on the mossy stones and munching our sandwiches while the finches fluttered in the yew trees above our heads, and five black and white cows gazed at us, fascinated, over the fence.

'I like picnicking in a churchyard,' said my aunt. 'It is peaceful. One is undisturbed. And there are seats and tables provided.' We repacked the basket, scattered the remaining crumbs for the birds, checked that no litter was left among the stones and continued on our way.

It was late in the afternoon before we reached the vicinity of Glencoppaleen. By then, I was trying to guide us with the road-map, but could not find the village marked. 'We'll ask the next person we come across,' I suggested.

'No.' My aunt was firm. 'We don't want to tell *everyone* our business.'

'What is our business?' I demanded, for in spite of all the veiled hints I felt I was being left somewhat in the dark.

My aunt did not reply. She merely said, 'This is it!' and turned the car so sharply off the road that I nearly fell over.

Bumping over ruts and splashing through the puddles of a narrow boreen, we reached the village; if we had blinked, we would have missed it. There were only three houses and a pub, the buildings long and low and thickly thatched. Grass was sprouting from the roofs and the walls were padded with cushions of moss, which softened their outline and made them look as if they were turning into little green hills. There was no one about. I thought the place must be deserted until I saw a cat lapping at a saucer of milk beside a door, and a row of bright washing flapping on a line.

We drove on and came to a halt outside another cottage, half a mile beyond the village. This dwelling was very different from its neighbours. Spotless white paint gleamed on its walls, and the thatch had been trimmed to make it look as if it had just returned from the barber's. An evergreen hedge had been clipped into forms of cockerels and hares, the lawn might have been smoothed with a rolling-pin, and the delphiniums and lupins were like a guard of honour lining the path up to the door.

'Dear Major! Always so proper!' murmured my aunt with a smile. She blew huskily on the bugle hanging by the door, which was opened almost immediately by a tall elderly man with a military moustache.

'Emmeline!' he exclaimed. 'Good to see you! Though, I

must say, you're a little late.' He consulted a watch on a chain. 'Tea is scheduled for seventeen-hundred hours. Will you come through and admire the garden? Or had we better get down to the business in hand?'

'First things first, I think, Major,' replied my aunt. 'We will be pleased to admire your garden later.'

'Very well, then. I'll just get my glass.'

He retreated into the house, leaving us standing on the well-scrubbed doorstep, and returned carrying a cap, a walking-stick, and a slim brass telescope, which he handed to me. 'Quick! March!' he said.

We walked briskly along the boreen between high hedges abrim with birds until we came to a stile. The view from the stile was of rolling green fields, dipping towards a little wooded valley. It was very peaceful. Water bubbled somewhere. Larks were singing in the blue sky overhead. 'There it is,' said the Major. 'Soon to be drowned beneath the wave.'

'Will they never learn?' murmured my aunt. 'And all for a few volts of electricity! I prefer oil lamps, myself.'

'The village is to go as well, you know,' Major Fitzwilliam Harker informed her. 'They are providing the inhabitants with council houses. I ask you! *Our* people—in a council estate! Still—they are not what they were.' He sighed.

'Oh, Major!' My aunt looked shocked. 'That means ... your house ...?'

He shrugged. 'I can always move camp,' he said. 'It's the Herd that worries me. What are we going to do about them? There they are—look!' He pointed to a lush field across the valley.

'I don't see anything,' I said, staring hard.

'Use the glass,' said the Major.

I raised the telescope, turning the eye-piece to adjust it to my sight. All I could see was pretty coloured patterns, such as one finds in a toy kaleidoscope. 'I still can't see,' I said.

'Look beyond the pattern,' said the Major.

With difficulty I focussed my eye between the petals of a gorgeous blue, green, and orange flower, and the meadow swung into my view, so plainly that I could make out the buttercups and daisies in the grass. Quite apart from each individual animal that grazed there.

'What beautiful little ponies!' I exclaimed.

'Not ponies. Look again.' Major Fitzwilliam Harker's sunburnt hand reached over to readjust the glass.

As he did so, a strong breeze stirred the meadow-grass, teasing the buttercups and daisies round the ponies' fetlocks. Like one animal, they all raised their heads and began to move, breaking into a bouncing trot that soon changed to a canter and became a gallop.

'Oh!' I cried. 'Their feet aren't touching the ground.'

'Probably not,' replied the Major. 'They don't, you know—when they are feeling happy.'

He had barely spoken when the nearest pony wheeled towards us, bucking and prancing, and tossing its thick mane to reveal what had been hidden by its forelock.

I dropped the glass and stared at the Major in disbelief. 'Why . . . they're not ponies,' I gasped. 'They're . . .'

He nodded. 'Unicorns—yes. The last unicorns in the western world. This is one of the few habitats that suits them. And the Government has taken it into its head to build a dam and flood the valley to provide electric power.'

'But they must be stopped.'

The Major grunted. 'Easier to cry "Halt" to a rogue elephant.'

'You cannot put a protection-order on something that you don't believe in,' commented my aunt. 'Even *you* require a glass to see them.'

I grabbed the telescope and stared through the petals of the flower once more, gazing greedily at a sight that I had seen only in a book of fairy tales. The herd consisted of just eight animals—nine! A tiny black foal romped by the side of a milk-white mare. As yet, his horn was no more than a bead of amber on his forehead.

Now that I looked carefully, I wondered how I could have mistaken them for ponies. Their coats were brighter; they seemed to give off some sort of glow. Each animal was cloven-hoofed ('Fissiped,' said my aunt) and bearded. As they tossed their heads in the wind, the single horn upon their foreheads stood out quite plainly; golden and twisted, like those old-fashioned sticks of barley-sugar you can still purchase at some chemists. The horn of the stallion (the one who had bucked and first revealed their identity) must have been fully two foot in length. The predominant colour of the herd was white, as I had seen them in illustrations. But some were piebald, and the foal was pure black.

'Oh, they're beautiful,' I murmured. 'We've *got* to save them.'

Tea in the Major's garden was a muted affair. Despite the hot toasted scones, the ample supply of fresh bread-and-butter, the rich fruit-cake and the chocolate biscuits, we were all drowned in gloomy thought.

'There's nothing for it,' sighed the Major. 'They'll have to be moved.'

'Where?'

'I was thinking—perhaps to Gortnadereen?'

My aunt shook her head. 'They've turned it into a forest-park,' she said. 'It's overrun by people and dogs every weekend.'

'Clonmeela, then?'

'A housing-estate,' said my aunt flatly.

'Well—' the Major sounded as if he was looking for suggestions.

'We have no choice but to take them north—to Inishnallis.'

The silence stretched like a piece of elastic.

'It's a long journey,' said the Major. 'How do we get them there?'

'There are not many of them. Couldn't we hire a horse-van?' I suggested.

'Unicorns and motor-vehicles don't mix,' the Major replied. 'They are allergic to the petrol fumes. Besides, they are liable to melt away when you put a roof over their heads. Remember what happened to the pair that chap Noah took into the Ark.'

'What did happen?' I asked.

My aunt pressed her lips together. 'We don't talk about it,' she said.

'Oh come now, Emmeline,' chided the Major, 'it's common knowledge.' He turned to me. 'Sea-foam,' he explained. 'Have you never seen the white horses on the waves?'

'Of course I have,' I said, trying to remember if I had

spotted their golden horns.

'To get back to the point,' continued the Major. 'We can't transport them. We'll have to drive them.'

'Drive!' exclaimed my aunt. 'You can't *drive* unicorns. They will only follow.'

'Follow what?' The Major became gloomier than ever. 'And there could be a problem when we reach Inishnallis,' he remarked. 'It isn't always there.'

'Major!' said my aunt sharply. 'This is not like you. You are retreating before Despair.' She rose from her seat. 'Jennifer and I must return home, or Tripitaka and Squew-wiff will complain that we starve them. We will put our heads together and do some thinking. I will be in touch with you very soon.'

'The usual channel of communication?' enquired the Major, as he escorted us to the gate.

'Of course.'

3. Hints of a Plot

*In which Mr. Potts is shown to be even
more sinister than suspected; and to have equally
unpleasant allies.*

The next day, much to my aunt's annoyance, the bees
swarmed.

'Stupid creatures! Just as we were busy thinking,' she
stormed. Grabbing hat, veil, gloves, and a large wickerwork
basket, she piled them on to the back of her bicycle, and
pedalled off in pursuit. Leaving me alone in the garden with
Squiff.

I finished the run I was making for him on the lawn,
popped him inside, and sat idly rocking on the swing.
Tripitaka had disappeared on private business of his own. An
unpleasant stench was wafting over the wall from the next-
door garden, where the chemist had lit one of his bonfires.

'Why does Mr. Potts burn all his household rubbish?' I
had asked my aunt one day. 'He is too ashamed to put it
in the dustbin,' had been the reply.

The stench was growing worse. 'No wonder the bees left
home,' I thought. I went into the house and shut all the
windows.

It was hot in the house. I finished reading the last few
pages of *Monkey*, which my aunt had kindly lent me (to
explain Tripitaka) and returned it to the shelves in the dining-
room which she kept her favourite books.

'I wonder if she would mind my borrowing something
else?' I thought, running my fingers along the spines of the
much-loved volumes, with their linen and paper covers so

worn by use that it felt like touching fraying satin. The leather-bound books were stronger. Fingering them, I imagined, was rather like stroking a snake, a mixture of rough and smooth. They were cool, rich, and exotic, with gold lettering. Their pages smelt faintly of spice.

Aunt Emm's tastes in reading were varied. She owned the best children's books I have ever read, a few books of poetry, some on natural history (especially wild-flowers), and a great many containing fairy-tales and legends. There were odd books in foreign languages which I could not read, and slim, much-thumbed volumes which I took at first to be cookery-books, but which turned out to contain recipes for medicines made with herbs. There were picture-books, and books with print so small that it made you squint.

'What's this?' My hand had fallen on an old brown battered-leather volume, with faded title printed gold on red:

IGNACEOUS LUCILUS—A BOOKE OF BEASTES

Being the description of All Creatures
here on Earthe and under the Seas and in the Heavens;
Common & Fabulous; Humble & Greate

'Common and fabulous!' I exclaimed. 'Perhaps it includes unicorns.'

I sat on the floor, turning the pages: Cameleoparde—Carp—Cat—Dragon—Dumbledore—Mammoth—Mouse—Oiliphant—Serpent . . . U—Unicorn!

A small horse, very fleete of foote, and shy, living in desert places, far from the haunt of Man. It has the beard of a goat, the cloven foote of a stag and, moste particular of all, a single, straight horne in the centre of its foreheade; which horne, some say, is made of Golde, some of Silver, others of Cinnabar, or Ivory. This horne, when powdered, gives Strength and Protection to the bearer, and is a powerful antidote to Poison.

Underneath, was a rough black and white woodcut of an animal rather like a donkey, with splayed toes, and a horn; 'So long that it would overbalance him,' I thought. '*Not* very flattering!'

I closed the book and sat, cross-legged, in thought. The room seemed to grow hotter; smells from Mr. Potts's bonfire seeped through the cracks round the windows and down the chimney.

'I'll go for a walk,' I thought. 'I need some fresh air. It will help me to think.'

The fishermen were out along the banks of the Canal, each standing like a sentinel beside his taut line, contemplating nothing while he waited. Some way apart from the main group, on the opposite bank, I caught sight of a familiar small figure with ginger whiskers. Apparently he was off duty; he was wearing a battered tweed hat with a frayed brim which had colourful fishing-flies stuck in the crown of it. He did not acknowledge my wave, being engrossed in the baiting of his hook.

'I wonder if he lives nearby,' I thought. 'I must ask Aunt Emm. But I don't suppose she'll tell me.'

I walked on, along the tow-path, thinking about the unicorns. What were they doing in a valley in County Wexford, being looked after by a funny old major—the *Ignaceous Lucilus* book said they lived in the desert? How had my aunt come to know about them? Well, that was easy! She and the Major seemed to be old friends; they even used the same sign—a hare (whatever that meant). Why were the unicorns in such danger? Surely they could just be moved to higher ground when the valley was flooded? As it seemed that only my aunt and the Major could see them, unaided, did it really matter where they went? Why did they have to be taken to some far-away island which, I had found on consulting the atlas, was *not* marked on the map? Neither was Glencoppaleen.

My thoughts were getting me nowhere. I turned and retraced my steps. This time, as I drew level with the little man he looked up and winked.

Aunt Emm had not returned; neither had Trip. I wandered about the house restlessly. The smoke from Mr. Potts's bonfire was dying down, but the smell lingered.

'I think I'll take the bus into town; look at the shop-windows,' I decided.

I fetched my purse, wrote a note for my aunt, checked that Squiff was quite safe, and left the house once more.

Close by the bus-stop stood the newsvendor's kiosk where we bought our papers. If there was one person I disliked, apart from Mr. Potts, it was Mr. Behan. He was a huge, fat man, with very little hair and rolls of pink flesh at the back of his head protruding over his collar. He had small piggy eyes and a husky voice that wheezingly repeated the title of the newspaper you asked for. He always called one 'Darlin'. 'The Herald? There ye are, me Darlin'.' And all the while his piggy eyes would be piercing you like two pins.

Eamonn Vincent Leonard—those were his names I had been told. E.V.L. 'Evil,' I thought. Imagine my dismay therefore when, on approaching the kiosk, I saw this gentleman in earnest conversation with the chemist. As I stood at the bus-stop (wishing that I was thin enough to hide behind it) I could not help overhearing some of what was said.

'The whole valley will be flooded,' the newsman wheezed.

'Then—*they* will be destroyed?' Mr. Potts sounded pleased.

'Undoubtedly!' Mr. Behan did his best to nod (which was difficult, with his rolls of fat and triple-chins). 'They cannot swim. The cloven-hoofed ones can't, my brother says. Pigs cut their own throats in their struggles, he tells me.' He wheezed disgustingly (*his* way of laughing), and made a cruel gesture with his podgy hand.

Mr. Potts was displaying increasing interest in the subject. 'Will you contact your brother?' he enquired.

'I will. The carcasses are bound to float up to the surface.'

I was, by this time, frozen with horror; stiff as the metal post I stood by. It was not necessary to hear Mr. Potts's next remark to know that they were talking about the unicorns.

'I want their horns,' he said greedily. 'I'll give you any price.'

Just then, the bus came along and I clambered aboard with relief. I felt, rather than saw, them watching me, and as I put out my hand to flag it down I overheard Mr. Potts say, '*Her* niece,' and the newsvendor's wheezing laugh. 'Bejapers! A spy in the camp!' he sneered.

I sat in the bus with my heart flapping at my ribs like a sheet in the wind. These people surely could not be involved in the flooding of the valley ... yet certainly, they knew about the unicorns and wished them ill! Mr. Behan, it seemed, had an equally unpleasant brother; a butcher by trade, perhaps? I wished I had not taken the bus into town. I wanted, desperately, to talk the matter over with my aunt.

I got off at the city centre, and wandered aimlessly. I looked at the shop windows, but was hardly conscious of what there was behind the glass. As if guided by some quirk of fate, I found myself standing outside the chemist's shop.

Eughan Potts
M.P.S.I: B.E.A: B.S.R: M.M.

The letters jumped up and down dizzily before my eyes. Mr. Potts would still be occupied at the kiosk, gossiping with his friend. I entered the shop.

It was a strange mixture of the old and the new. Great glass bottles of colourful liquids, which I supposed must contain coloured water, were ranged along a high shelf, and behind the counter there were tiers of little mahogany drawers with bone or ivory handles. The contents of each were labelled in black and gold print: ESS. OF…TINCT. OF…THE OINT.

The rest of the shop was very up to date, with shiny glass counters and stands displaying the usual wares one finds in a chemist's; corn-plasters; bottles of cough-mixture; toothbrushes; tubes of ointment; beauty-preparations. I was drawn to one counter where Mr. Potts's own special remedies were on offer—herbal skin tonic, indigestion-tablets, cure for acne. Each was described by a label written in thin spidery handwriting which I guessed was Mr. Potts's own. Certain words were underlined: *Natural* product; *Fresh* herbs; *Pure* animal-fat…

Suddenly, I felt sick. I knew, for certain, the use Mr. Potts made of all those guinea-pigs and mice! I didn't want to think what happened behind the closed doors of those windowless sheds. To try to distract myself, I moved over to a small stand bearing an assortment of what were termed, coyly, 'Tints for the hair'.

'He dyes his hair, too!' I said savagely, out loud, looking at a phial of syrupy blue-black substance and recalling Mr. Potts's unnaturally black hair sleeked round his pasty face, and his equally dark toothbrush moustache.

'Can I help you?'

The words froze the atmosphere like ice. I had not heard Mr. Potts's assistant enter from the small dispensary at the back of the shop, but I fancied she must have been watching me for some time. She was one of those women who are neither young nor old, with a face so heavily made-up that she looked like a cross between a badly painted doll and a clown. Despite the heavy outlines and the false curling lashes, I could not help noticing that her eyes were as pale and as watery as Mr. Potts's. They were regarding me with dislike and distrust. 'Can I help you?' she repeated.

'No, thank you. I'm just looking,' I said politely.

The pale eyes narrowed, and the long painted fingernails

dug into the neat white paper-package she was carrying. 'Mr. Potts does *not* encourage loiterers,' she stated coldly, her scarlet mouth twitching at the corner.

'That's all right, then.' I ceased to be polite. 'For I'm just going. You can tell Mr. Potts that I wouldn't buy any of his poisons, anyway,' I threw over my shoulder as I ran out of the shop.

Anger and loathing swept me along to the bus terminal, and on to the bus. The newsvendor's kiosk was closed and shuttered, I noticed as I passed. I wondered what he and Mr. Potts were doing.

I found my aunt tired and dispirited, for she had been unable to catch the bees. As I made her a cup of tea, I related the happenings of the afternoon.

'It was foolish to be rude,' Aunt Emm commented. 'That man is very dangerous... Eughan! The Yew! The most deadly tree in the wood,' she added, half to herself. 'Poisonous in bark, and leaf, and seed ...'

'He's only a chemist,' I argued.

My aunt put down her cup. '*Only* a chemist! BACHELOR OF ENCHANTMENT AND ALCHEMY: BACHELOR OF SORCERIAL RESEARCH: *MASTER MAGICIAN,*' she said slowly.

I whistled. 'So, that's what the letters mean!' I said.

'You see what we're up against,' said my aunt.

At that moment a sound shrilled through the house, and we both went to the door. The little man looked so ridiculous in hat and veil that I almost laughed.

'He has found the bees. They are safe under the basket,' my aunt said, after listening to his grunts.

'That little man is very useful. He's always popping up,' I chuckled as we closed the door.

My aunt smiled. 'He is a wearer of many hats,' she said.

4. The Weaver of the Winds

In which Jennifer goes underground;
finds herself in the presence of a Blind Power;
and receives two gifts.

My aunt and I made pounds of strawberry jam, with the fruit bought from growers by the side of the way on our return from Wexford. As we watched the ruby liquid bubble in the great copper preserving-pan, we kept our promise to the Major, put our heads together, and talked. Naturally I asked her about the unicorns.

'Certainly, unicorns did exist in Ireland,' she explained. The word 'desert' in the book simply meant 'wild places'. Magic was spread throughout the world, though there were times (and this was one of them) when it was somewhat 'thin on the ground'.

'Once there were herds of unicorn in all four provinces,' she continued. 'Now they have dwindled to those few you saw hidden in the valley. Little was known of them, of course. They were always difficult to find, being timid and avoiding all contact with Man. Only a young girl might touch one, and then she would need the Sight to see it. Nevertheless, they were there; minding their own business, like many another creature.

'Not any more! Man is such a meddler! And, when he meddles, he destroys. All the unicorns' old grazing-grounds have gone; planted, row upon row, with spruce and fir to turn into chip-board and sheets of paper; smothered by smart new houses; or simply tidied into amusement-parks.'

'Is that why we have to take them so far?' I asked.

33

'Part of the reason, yes. It is not going to be an easy task, either, even when we find the way to do it. The few remaining animals are unstable (you saw, yourself, how they are no longer even pure in colour). They may vanish altogether during the journey. Or, they may simply complete a process already started, and change into ordinary ponies... Now you tell me, to make matters worse, that the Opposition are on our trail. It is serious. We could do with some advice.'

I would have liked to ask Aunt Emm what she meant by 'the Opposition'. But, at that moment, the strawberries threatened to boil over and she declared the jam to be set.

With the jam in its jars, and my aunt occupied in thinning out the lettuce, I volunteered to take Tripitaka for his walk. 'Provided you behave yourself,' I told him. He blinked, disdainfully.

To my surprise, on turning in the direction of the Canal I found the post-box on the corner (I had supposed that it appeared only when we wanted to post a letter). The door in the side for the postman to collect the mail was wide open, and the little man was sitting in the aperture, smoking a clay pipe. When he saw me he stood up, knocked out his pipe with a ringing sound on the wall of the box and, stepping forward, doffed his hat, which I noticed was a tricorn one such as footmen wear on special occasions. He made me a most stately bow, then taking me by the hand, led me into the box.

'Where are we going?' I asked anxiously, trying to withdraw my hand. The little man merely held it tighter.

A flight of stone steps spiralled downwards. For some while our way was lit from the door at the top, still standing open. By and by, however, it grew pitch-dark. The little man stopped with a grunt. Without letting go my hand, he fumbled in his pocket and produced a sparkler. There was no need for matches; he merely waved it in the air until it flared to life. Guided by the flickering fizzing firework we continued to descend. Tripitaka, whose lead I had dropped in my alarm, seemed to know where he was going, for he flowed down the stairs in front of us like liquid honey.

We reached the bottom and found ourselves looking down a long corridor, lit on either side by small lights tucked into the shells of snails. Glancing up as we walked along, I saw that we were passing under those gratings in the street where water flows down from the gutter; a bicycle, spinning by overhead, sent a shower of mud pattering on my shoulders. In one place a coin fell, landing with a clink at my feet.

'Where are we going?' I asked the little man again. He only grunted.

The corridor came to an end at last, outside a solid oak door studded with nails. Dropping my hand, the little man produced a key and standing on tip-toe fitted it into the lock. With much puffing and kicking, he swung on it until it turned. Caught by a draught on the far side, the door flew open with such force that he was knocked all of a heap on to the floor, and Trip and I found ourselves being sucked inward by the gale and flung against the lower treads of a flight of stairs; fortunately for us, it was thickly carpeted. Urged on by the little man, who was clutching at his hat, we crawled slowly to the top.

A heavy tapestry curtain covering a doorway whispered and soughed in the breeze. From behind it came a sound that was both rhythmical and faintly familiar: 'Whoosh-and-clonk! Whoosh-and-clonk!' The little man lifted the curtain, and we passed gratefully into the calm beyond.

The room was round like the inside of a drum. At intervals windows, set high in the wall, sent shafts of light slanting on floor and furnishings, causing everything to be patched in bright or dusky colour. The sound we had heard came from the working of a wooden loom, where a thin elderly man was seated. His long fingers, caught by a shaft of sunlight as they busily sent the shuttle to and fro, were pale as ivory; his

silvery hair was tumbling round his shoulders; his eyes were
brilliant blue. I knew at once, without being told, that he was
blind.... The wind whined in the chimney, and gently
fluttered the feathers of a starling and a long-eared owl,
perched on a rail behind him. The little man grunted, bowed,
and withdrew.

'I thank you, Nutmouse,' said the blind man. (I realised
that he must be his master.)

I was shamed by Trip's lack of manners. Leaping over the
loom and sending spools of yarn spinning across the floor,
he landed upon the blind man's knee. The treadle jerked to
a stop; the shuttle jammed; the starling ruffled his feathers
and lectured raucously, while the owl registered his
disapproval by raising his ear-tufts like railway signals and
shooting a pellet of mouse bones across the room.

'Sails fall slack; a fine yacht is becalmed,' commented the man. His slender hands felt for Tripitaka's head, and rubbed him behind the ears. Noisily, the cat began to purr.

'Thunder!' exclaimed the blind man. He smiled.

'I'm sorry. He really is a dreadful cat.' I replaced the spools. 'What are you weaving?'

'South-westerlies—the tossers and soakers. I apologise for the draught on the stairway. Anyway, it is time for a change.' He reached for a large pair of scissors and snipped off the thread.

I moved from perusing the intricate pattern of smoky-blues and greys upon the loom to examine the hangings on the wall. The shapes were spirals, like those carved on ancient stones, undulations and curlicues such as I had seen decorating the letters in the Book of Kells. The colours reminded one of the creamy tips of waves—a swirl of dust—leaves dancing in the breeze. All the outward signs of... 'You weave the Winds!' I cried.

'That's right.' The blind man tucked the purring cat underneath his arm, and came to join me. 'That one is from the North; you can feel the flakes of snow. This, from the balmy South. A Hurricane—one of my best! Trade winds!' Unable to see his work, he touched each piece with loving fingers.

The hanging above the fireplace did not represent a wind. It was a small green banner on which had been woven a white hare, very similar to that which hung on a chain about my aunt's neck and to the engraving on the ring I had noticed on the Major's finger as he had reached out to adjust the telescope. But this hare wore a golden crown around his neck.

I think the Weaver must have sensed that I was looking at it, for he set Trip on the floor, and reaching for a bottle from the shelf poured out two glasses of amber wine. Handing one to me, he motioned me to sit upon the settle by the fireplace.

'"The Company of the Hare" are worried,' he remarked. 'There's trouble in the world outside.'

'They want to flood the valley of Glencoppaleen,' I told him. 'The unicorns will drown.'

'I know,' he nodded. 'I cannot see, but I hear things. Messages come to me down the chimney. And my friends'— he indicated the starling and the owl—'bring me news.'

'What's to be done? My aunt says they should go to Inishnallis, but we don't know how to get them there.'

'The grazing's good. If you can find it,' commented the Weaver.

'The Major's very depressed. He says it's a long journey. He seems unsure of the way.'

'You will need guidance.'

The Weaver stood up. As he did so a gale hit the side of the house, bursting the catch on one of the windows so that it clapped sharply shut and open. The birds took off in alarm, circling the room in and out amongst the billowing hangings until they sought safety upon the chimney-breast. Nutmouse appeared with a long pole to close the window, but before he could do so his master stayed his hand. Standing with his silver locks blown backwards, his bright sightless eyes seemed to scan the flapping pane. 'Tell me,' he asked, 'could you face that wind?'

I did not understand the reason for his question. 'I . . . suppose so,' I answered slowly.

'Come, then.'

He led me to a door I had not noticed earlier and, taking a key from a chain on his belt, unlocked it. Immediately, it was blown violently open by the wind. He took my hand, and we stepped outside.

The building, I saw, was one of those Martello towers set on a rise. On one side there was a view down a slope on to the roofs of the City, and on the other one could look out to sea. The railed iron walkway we stood on spanned the

outside of the tower. Looking up, I noticed a twisting iron staircase mounting to the roof, upon the flat floor of which a tall tiled steeple had been added. At its summit, a weather-vane in the shape of a winged horse veered about in the breeze. 'You must fetch that down. You will find it useful,' said the Weaver.

I hesitated. The Weaver's hand on my shoulder propelled me gently forward. I began to climb.

At each step, the staircase shivered and bucked like a frightened beast. I dared not look down for fear of losing my nerve, but kept my face turned resolutely towards the wind. It had begun to rain, and cold droplets stung my forehead, pasting themselves chillingly to my hair. My progress was not helped by the fact that Tripitaka had skipped up the stairs in my wake, and was now nudging me from behind.

We reached the roof in a bedraggled state. I stood contemplating the steeple despondently, while the wind spun, snarling, about my ears, trying to force me back the way I had come.

'I could never get up there,' I thought. 'And, even if I did, the weather-vane is too heavy to bring down.'

What seems impossible to a girl may be attempted by a cat! Scattering raindrops from his sodden coat, Tripitaka hurled himself at the steeple, and claws scritching upon the slippery tiles proceeded to scramble upward as if he was climbing a tree.

'Trip! Stop! You'll fall!' I shrieked. But the wind caught my voice and blew it out to sea.

The cat had reached the peak of the pinnacle. Craning my neck, I could see him crouching by the flying-horse. He was patting at it with his paw as if it was a toy.

'Oh, Trip, come down. Stop playing silly games.'

All of a sudden the weather-vane came loose. It was plummeting towards me like a stone! I leapt aside, put out a hand to shield myself, and . . .

And caught a tiny metal flying-horse!

It was beautiful—a little round compass in a richly ornamented frame marked 'N-E-S-W'! The white enamelled horse with ruby eyes and golden wings pranced at its centre; his eyes, which flashed like lightning, the colour of sunrise— sunset. Whichever way I twisted the compass he spun to face me, his flowing tail pointing towards the North.

Tripitaka was weaving his triumph round my feet. The wind had dropped. Together, we descended with the compass.

'Well done!' said the Weaver.

'It wasn't really me,' I admitted. 'Trip...'

'You *tried*,' said the Weaver gently. 'Now you have something to show you the way. But you will also need something to guide the unicorns.'

We went back indoors. The Weaver crossed to the fireplace, and putting his hand up the chimney felt around. He brought down a slender silver flute. When he blew upon it, there came the sound of the wind whispering in the grass, a night-breeze plucking at the surface of a pool.

'How wonderful!' I laughed.

He pressed the flute into my hand. 'They cannot be driven, but they will follow,' he reminded me. 'Good luck! Fair winds go with you. Nutmouse! Guide them home.'

'What *have* you got there?' my aunt demanded when we returned home.

And, when I showed her...

'Well! Well! You were fortunate. He seldom receives visitors, nowadays.'

5. Silver Feet

*In which the journey is begun; almost
comes to a premature end; and a useful recruit
joins the ranks.*

My aunt visited the bank and had a long discussion with her
bank manager. We bought a shining silver caravan, just big
enough for two, with a bright little stove at one end, shelves
and cupboards to put things in, a table fastened firmly to the
floor, and two bunks, with room under one for Tripitaka's
basket. (As it happened, he slept *on* the bunk for the entire
journey!) Squiff's cage fitted neatly into an alcove as if
purpose-built. We packed all the clothes we thought we
would need, stowed tins of food at the kitchen end, and filled
the shelves with books. Aunt Emm took the bees for their
holiday early that year. We sent a note to my parents:

> Have gone on a tour. Will post cards from our various
> stopping-places. See you when we get back. Do not worry.
> Love, etc . . .

We locked the house, hid the key, and set off for Wexford.

We found the Major in full battle dress, packing a kit-bag.
A khaki tent was spread out on the lawn to air. His spirits
rose when I showed him the Weaver's compass. He spent the
next few days behind the closed door of his study, examining
maps and weather-charts and planning the route. At last he
declared that all was ready. 'Operation Unicorn' could begin.
  First, however, he felt it necessary to 'brief' the villagers.
Summoned by bugle, they shuffled up the garden path and

clustered respectfully round the door, while the Major stood upon the step to address them. I was struck by how few of them there were, and how great the average age! Nobody looked younger than sixty-five, and one old woman must have been at least a hundred.

'My men,' began the Major. (The ancient crone tittered and nudged her neighbour.) 'My men,' glowering at the old lady, 'I have called you here for a very serious reason. As you know, the Company of the Hare is to be disbanded. Weakened by many a fray, we are forced to give way before an army of greater numbers and superior equipment. Before you are pensioned off, put out to grass I would rather say,' (cheers from a couple of greybeards as they stood stiffly to attention, their eyes gleaming) 'you will have one more duty to perform. I have a last order to give: GUARD OUR FLANKS!

'This is no rout. We withdraw in *honourable* retreat, strong in the knowledge that one day we will reform. It is imperative, in the meantime, that the Rare Ones should be saved. I call upon you to guard the secret of our destination. The Enemy has many spies. Remember "Careless talk costs lives". Company DISMISS!'

The bugle sounded the 'last post'. Gnarled hands were raised to wrinkled foreheads in salute, and the old ones departed to their doomed village.

'What will happen to them?' I asked. 'Who *are* the Company of the Hare? How can they possibly "guard our flanks"? They look so old and weak. That old lady was about a hundred.'

'As a matter of fact, she is three hundred and seventy-five. Quite a youngster. But, under the circumstances, she has not worn well, poor soul.'

My aunt must have seen from my face that I didn't know whether to believe her or not. She took a large silk handkerchief from her sleeve and blew her nose. 'You ask too many questions,' she snapped. 'There is much that you simply would not understand. But, I'll tell you this; those people may be old, but they are stronger than they look. All the same, it will be necessary for us to leave as soon as possible.'

We left that night, at midnight.

We planned to travel at night, partly as the Major said, 'For security reasons,' and partly, as my aunt pointed out, because the unicorns were stronger and more lively in the night hours. Also they were, as I realised to my delight, visible without the use of the Major's telescope, even to me.

'You go first.' My aunt gave me a push. 'Play the Weaver's flute and they will follow.'

'But,' I protested, 'I haven't had much practise. I can only play two tunes. Which shall it be?'

'Don't bother with a tune. Just blow,' said Aunt Emm.

I put the flute to my lips and took a deep breath. A strange noise came out. It sounded like a barn-owl.

'Wrong bird,' said my aunt. 'Hardly enticing to the unicorns. Try again.'

I blew more gently and was rewarded by a liquid stream of notes, mellow and beautiful; bird song such as I had never heard before.

'What's that?' I stopped, amazed at my own prowess.

'A nightingale!' cried my aunt joyfully. 'I haven't heard one since I was in Isfahan. Play it again.'

I did as I was told. The unicorns raised their heads, and whinnied.

We must have made a quaint cavalcade as we wound our way through the sleeping countryside, keeping to the less-frequented roads, and whenever possible following foot-paths across the fields or stealing up the silent bridle-paths through the woods. First marched the Major, map-case and compass in hand, his swagger-stick tucked beneath his arm, and his gun-holster at his belt. Later, I was to discover that the latter held nothing but a bag of bull's-eyes! For all his rapped orders and army jargon the Major was very strictly a Man of Peace. ('He holds the "Star of Peace",' my aunt told me. 'There is no higher award than that.')

I followed, blowing from time to time upon the Weaver's flute to encourage the unicorns. They moved in erratic fashion, led by the stallion who made frequent stops to snuff the moonlit air. The mares were skitterish. They shied at shadows; they hesitated before puddles, sniffing suspiciously and beating a tattoo upon the ground with uncertain hoofs; they leapt the bank to sample delicacies growing in the ditch. The foal took the whole excursion for a game, and caused his mother much anxiety by dancing to and fro beyond her reach.

My aunt's old car brought up the rear, its roof-rack and the top of the caravan piled high with the Major's 'equipment' and emergency rations for the unicorns, for they were particularly partial to a mix of wild thyme and a certain rare orchid, which we did not suppose we would find upon our journey. Trip presided over the baggage like a prince, while inside the caravan Squew-wiff could be heard squeaking in protest whenever my aunt drove over a bump.

Progress was slow. Unaccustomed to travelling, the unicorns were hard to manage. At one point the stallion dug in his toes and refused to follow our chosen path, forcing us to make a detour. The foal grew tired, and we were obliged to stop at regular intervals to let him rest. Matters were not improved when the Major got muddled with his map-reading, and led us for several miles in the wrong direction. Fortunately, the frantic spinning of the Weaver's compass alerted him to his mistake.

At last, with the dawn breeze whispering in the trees and our eyes leaden from lack of sleep, we came upon a spot where a brook chattered over stones and a clump of rowans, still thick with flowers of clotted cream, shielded a small expanse of grass from the inquisitive upon the road.

'The Quickenberry!' exclaimed my aunt. 'The Tree of Life. We will be quite safe here.'

We drew in, off the road, and set up camp. The unicorns wandered down to the brook to drink. Soon, there was a delicious smell of frying as eggs sizzled in a pan above a crackling fire.

'Let's overlook the washing-up,' said my aunt, when we had eaten. 'Time for bed.'

I was awakened in the late afternoon by Squew-wiff's piercing demands for food. He had munched his way through the carrot and lettuce I had given him earlier, and was letting me know of his compelling need for grass. I tumbled off my bunk, transferred him to his grazing-pen and took him outside.

The Major was already up, out of his tent, and list in hand was checking the baggage on top of the caravan. There was no sign of the unicorns. I was about to express my concern when something soft as thistledown touched my forehead and warm breath was blown into my ear.

'Of course! You're there, even if I can't see you,' I said. I sat on the grass, watching Squiff nibble and bob and listening to the soft sounds of my unseen companions as they moved around me.

The sun sank behind the trees. Gradually, the unicorns became visible to my sight. First as vapours of white mist, then taking a more solid form as it grew dark. Dainty hoofs treading the blossom-strewn grass beneath the trees, tails swishing at the clouds of small midges rising from the stream, heads tossing (some white, some black and white, with dark gentle eyes like a fawn's); now and then a unicorn snorted before bending, with silken beard trailing, to crop the grass.

'I could stay here forever,' I thought.

But the moment passed. My aunt arose, and we busied ourselves with preparing supper. 'Our departure will be at twenty-two hundred hours,' announced the Major.

We had difficulty persuading the unicorns to leave the haven of the rowans. It took much puffing and blowing and many different bird-calls to encourage them on to the road. We were, according to our commander, 'Behind Schedule', as we set off for the hills.

The way grew steep. Loose stones rattled beneath our feet and bounced away behind us. A mean little wind whined over the hillside, and clouds went scudding across the moon; fat bloated clouds, casting shadows like dark blankets to smother the heather. They reminded me of Mr. 'Evil' Behan and a whole host of his brothers, blown up like balloons, speeding through the sky to blot us out. Even the Major's broad back in its army greatcoat lost its reassurance. I pulled up my collar

and, keeping my head low, fixed my eye upon the path.

The sharp bleeping of Aunt Emm's car-horn brought me to my senses. I turned to find that by neglecting to play the flute I had left the unicorns far behind. Heads down, noses almost brushing the earth, ears flat, they were struggling to follow. Every one, including the foal, was lame.

'Major! Stop! Look what's happened!'

Filled with remorse, I dashed back down the track. The herd ignored me. Dull-eyed, they hobbled on to the nearest patch of grass and stood motionless.

'A cavalry should never march without its farrier.' Tut-tutting beneath his moustache, the Major examined the damage.

'Tender feet!' he declared. The stallion, especially, was a pathetic sight with one foot badly swollen, a stone lodged in the cleft.

'Oh, I'm sorry.' Tears in my eyes, I placed my wet cheek against his white neck. He made no move, but I felt him shudder beneath my touch.

My aunt hurried to the caravan to fetch the first-aid kit, and some ointment. Feeling useless and ashamed, I crept away to be by myself.

Barely twenty-four hours on the road, and it seemed as if our journey had come to an end already! It was *my* fault. If only I had not walked so fast, had paid attention to the unicorns, and turned round sooner. Finding a huge granite boulder by the side of the way I scrambled up and perched, playing little snatches of the two tunes I knew upon the flute. The clouds had been blown away, and the moonlight gave the hillside a black-and-white look like a photograph. Here and there boulders, similar to the one upon which I sat, crouched amongst the heather like big white trolls. An owl flew by, white against the black; his cry was mournful.

I began to play a little nursery tune I had learnt when I was small:

> *Hob shoe, hob!*
> *Hob shoe, hob!*
> *Here's a nail, and there's a nail,*
> *And that's well shod!*
> *Hob shoe, hob . . .*

'What was that?' My music trailed to a stop.

The owl cried again. I looked around. The hillside was deserted. But somewhere, not far away, someone had picked up my melody and was whistling it!

> *Hob shoe, hob!*
> *Here's a nail, and there's a nail,*
> *And that's well shod.*

Round a bend in the road came marching a small figure with ginger whiskers. He had a flat cap pushed back upon his head and wore a blacksmith's leather apron, split to allow him to straddle a horse's leg. On his back, bouncing and clanging at every step, were strung a tiny anvil and a portable metal forge.

'Nutmouse!' I recalled the name the Weaver had given him, 'You are the very person we need.'

The owl hooted once more. It settled on a thorn-tree, adjacent to the road, shaking its feathers like someone settling the down in a quilt, and raising the two earlike tufts upon its head. 'I've seen you somewhere before,' I thought. But I had no time to ponder for, with a wink, Nutmouse had passed me by. I slid down off the rock, and followed.

On reaching the spot where my aunt and the Major were endeavouring to set up a makeshift camp, Nutmouse halted. Still whistling between his teeth, he took in the situation at a glance. Laying down his load, he unrolled a linen bundle to reveal hammer, tongs, pliers, hoof-pick, bellows—all the hardware of the blacksmith's craft. He grunted to me, signalling to fetch water in a bucket, and commenced to light the charcoal in the forge.

In no time the fire was hot. Nutmouse plucked a bar of silver from his apron pocket, and thrust it with the tongs between the coals.

'Hob shoe, hob!' Clang, clang, clink! Fizz-zzz, as the newly shaped metal was plunged into the bucket.

The stallion stood patient and uncomplaining. I wound my fingers in his mane, holding his horn while Nutmouse dislodged the stone and drove the tiny nails into his cloven hoof. Soon the whole herd, heads high, were frolicking on shining, silver-shod feet.

'Good man!' The Major was impressed. He clapped Nutmouse on the back, almost knocking him into the bucket. 'You're a useful chap. You'd better join the ranks and march with us.'

6. Travellers

In which there is an unforeseen
manifestation; and a meeting by the wayside
results in a disappearance.

Once over the Blackstairs Mountains, our journey became
easier. The nights were warm and balmy, filled with the
gentle sounds of birds shifting in their sleep and small animals
scuttering through the grassy verges; moths flitted like tiny
ghosts amongst the late flowers of the hawthorn. We passed
darkened villages and farms, seeing no one, only the cattle
clustered in groups beneath the shelter of trees, chewing
dreamily. Now and again a cat or a fox, out hunting, would
look at us with eyes that glowed like green embers, before
passing by on more pressing business. I became used to
walking long miles in the dark with Nutmouse, hands thrust
in pockets, striding silently at my side. The unicorns, grown
accustomed to the nightly journey, clip-clopped contentedly
behind us on their silver feet.

There was, however, a nagging worry.

It was a curious thing, but the further the unicorns
travelled from Glencoppaleen the more visible they became.
It was almost as if, with every mile, they were leaving behind
the World of Make-believe and Magic, and entering Reality.

'It is as I feared,' mourned my aunt. 'If this journey lasts
too long, they will all be changed into ordinary ponies.'

She was particularly concerned about one piebald mare,
larger than the others, who showed a tendency to manifest
herself to normal human sight in broad daylight. Always the
first to reappear (even before the sun set in the evening), her

stouter, cobby form—more black than white—could be seen
clearly long after her companions had faded to shadows,
vanishing with the dawn.

'This won't do at all,' lamented Aunt Emm. 'Jennifer
reported seeing her at eleven o'clock this morning. I could
swear her horn is shrinking, too. I've tried rubbing it with
coltsfoot leaves but they make no difference.'

'She'll settle,' said the Major placidly. 'She probably had
a fright along the way and it's upsetting her. You know how
changeable they are.'

She did not settle; if anything, she became worse. We
redoubled our efforts to seek out the little-known routes,
making sure we camped where nobody could see us. This was
becoming difficult, as we were trekking across the flat open
grasslands of County Kildare. It was inevitable that, one day,
morning would catch us with no cover but a thin windblown
hedge.

There was nothing we could do but make the most of it.
My aunt drove the caravan through a gate, and we set the
unicorns to graze as far away from the road as possible,
shielded by a wide sweep of gorse. We were just having
breakfast when a family of travellers arrived.

It was obvious that the broad verge on the far side of the
hedge was one of their regular stopping-places. They settled
on to it with the ease of long custom; the children falling
almost immediately to shying stones at an old tree trunk as
if picking up the game from the previous day; the dogs
greeting familiar scents with wagging tails. It did not take
them long to pitch their camp as their worldly goods consisted
only of a horse-drawn wagon (the old type with the barrel-
roof) and a rickety cart piled high with scrap on which was
perched a very old woman, as wrinkled and bent as a dried
oak-leaf (looking as fragile as a leaf, too; one puff of the wind,
I thought, would blow her away). In addition to the skewbald
in the shafts of the wagon, and the poor broken-kneed donkey

which struggled to pull the cart, they had three horses
running loose. They left their beasts to forage by the side of
the way while they draped a piece of canvas over a frame
to house the old woman, and set about building a fire and
hanging washing on the hedge. Then, they had leisure to
notice us!

I was scared. I do not know much about the travelling
people and could not help wondering if they would take us
for a rival gang on their territory, and attack us. We did not
look very prepossessing. With her untidy hair and loose-
fitting clothes, my aunt looked little better than a tramp;
Nutmouse must have appeared wild and strange and, after
walking the roads for so many nights, I knew I did not look
much better.

One glance at the Major, however, spruce and trim as he

sat polishing his gun-belt, must have convinced them that we
were not itinerants but tourists. There was some consultation.
A man could be seen giving orders to one of the women.
Presently, she appeared on our side of the hedge, wrapped
in a plaid rug and carrying a baby.

'Could you spare something for the little 'un, Ma-am?' she
begged my aunt. Aunt Emm dug into her pocket for 50p.
and a bag of toffees for the children. As she seemed inclined
to linger, the Major (always suspicious of those not as
regimented as himself) cleared his throat and she went away.
Except for a teenage girl, bearing a chipped teapot and asking
for a 'sup o' tea for the Granny', they left us in peace. The
two men of the party went off down the road in the direction
of the nearest town and they were followed some time later
by the woman with the baby. The teenage girl stirred
something in a pot over the fire; the granny snoozed at the
door of her tent.

It was one of their dogs which caused the trouble. A lean
mangy mongrel, he came sniffing around as we were
preparing for our daytime sleep. He found Trip seated in the
sun at the entrance of our caravan, regarding him with
loathing. Retreating several paces, he commenced to bark.
This brought the children, with shouts and sticks and stones.
Once they had driven the dog away, they remained to play
in the field.

There were four of them, two boys and two girls. They
pestered the Major with questions until he was driven to seek
cover in his tent. They pointed and giggled at Nutmouse,
forcing him to put a balaclava on his head and take a walk.
Seeing my aunt was already asleep in the caravan, they turned
their attention towards me.

The cat's paws were a funny colour! Had he burnt them?
They could not understand about his being Siamese.

'What's that?' demanded the younger boy, a stubby, sandy-
haired fellow of about eight, with a mischievous grin.

I did my best to explain, but he was not listening. Why, he wanted to know, were we taking a cat on holiday, anyway?

'Is that a mouse?'

The other boy (thin and dark, with an old man's face) had spotted Squiff nestling on my knee.

'Looks more like a rat,' said Sandy-hair gleefully. The youngest child, a little girl of four with a mop of curly red hair—very pretty—gave a scream.

'Ssh!' I said. 'It's all right. He's only a guinea-pig.'

'Funny sort of pig!' Sandy-hair doubled up with laughter. 'Wouldn't give much bacon.'

'Whist, Johnnie! You're frightening the poor beast.'

The elder girl (about my own age, I guessed) pushed the boys aside. Timidly, she stretched out her hand and stroked Squiff's nose with two fingers.

'He's a dote,' she said. 'Are you not scared the cat will get him?'

'Trip's very good. He wouldn't harm him.'

I looked up at the girl's serious grey eyes, her neatly plaited hair hanging down on either side of her pale thin face (did she get enough to eat, I wondered?) and liked her.

'You can hold him, if you like,' I said.

'Could I?' She smiled, her whole face lighting up, her grey eyes sparkling. Eagerly, she held out her hands.

'What's your name?' I asked, as I passed Squiff over. She had no chance to answer.

'That's a trim little horse!'

At once, all eyes were turned in the direction Johnnie was pointing. Appalled, I found myself withdrawing Squiff involuntarily and hiding him beneath my jersey. There, standing in broad daylight, calmly nibbling the yellow flowers from the gorse, was our big piebald mare.

She had faded with the others, earlier; I knew she had. Aunt Emm had sent me over to check. Now, apparently, something had gone wrong. She had reappeared.

'W-would you like to come in to see the inside of the caravan?' I stammered. Their entrance, I knew, would wake my aunt. But I had to draw the boys' attention away from the mare, somehow. 'Perhaps you'd like to see where Squiff lives,' I added shyly. I was painfully aware that I had hurt the girl's feelings by my sudden snatching of the guinea-pig, and I wanted to make it up to her.

Fortunately, at that moment, their teenage sister came to the gate of the field, shouting that the food was ready. Without a backward glance, the children turned and ran to her.

'Fade! For goodness sake, fade!' I muttered to the unicorn between my teeth. As if she could hear me, she shook her mane. It was true, what Aunt Emm had said—her horn was shrinking. As she walked away, I could have sworn that she was growing fainter and was about to disappear. Perhaps I should have alerted my aunt or the Major. But we had walked far that night, and I was tired. I decided to turn in.

I was awakened some time later by Nutmouse's grunts, as he tried to rouse my aunt.

'What is it, Nutmouse? What's the matter?' But, somehow I knew.

Nutmouse kept holding up his ginger fingers, counting them off one by one: 'One, two, three, four, five, six, seven, eight, nine!' The number of the unicorns. When he came to the ninth finger, however, he covered it with his other hand and shook his head.

'He says one of the unicorns is missing,' cried my aunt. Still clad in her red flannel nightie, she ran to the door.

'The big mare is not there,' she reported, shading her eyes. 'Have you searched the field?' She turned to Nutmouse.

He nodded, making large sweeping gestures, as if he had searched the whole wide world. My heart sank.

'I should have posted a sentry,' declared the Major when

he heard the news. 'I knew those travellers were not to be trusted. They'll be at the back of this, I bet.'

'Oh, surely not,' cried my aunt. 'I'll go and talk to them.'

But, when my aunt, with me running at her side, reached the road verge there was no one to be seen. Dogs, horses, donkey, caravan and cart—all were gone! The remains of the fire still smouldered, and one or two pieces of cloth, left behind, drooped like tattered flags upon the hedge.

'What now? I must warn the Major.' Dismayed, my aunt turned back into the field.

I lingered. I had seen something, more than a rag, beyond the hedge on the far side of the road. The travelling girl's faded cotton dress fluttered as she scrambled through.

'I waited,' she panted. 'The others have gone on. It's me Uncle Jack! He's a bad lot. Ma always said . . .'

'What do you mean?' I asked.

She glanced along the road as if she was frightened that someone might be listening, or, perhaps, she was merely in a hurry to be off.

'He's taken your little horse,' she said. 'The black and white one. He's going to sell it at the fair. I tried to stop him, but . . .' She flung her hands apart, helplessly.

'I understand,' I said. 'Where is the fair? And, when?'

'Today. The big town.' She pointed down the road. Already, she was starting to move away. 'You'll have to be quick,' she called over her shoulder.

'Thanks,' I shouted. Then, as an afterthought, 'What is your name?'

She stopped, standing in the middle of the road. 'It's Maggie,' she said awkwardly. 'What's yours?'

'Jenny,' I replied. ('Jennifer' suddenly sounded too pompous.)

''Bye, Jenny.' Waving her hand, she was off, feet clad in boots that were too big, slip-slapping as she ran along the road.

''Bye!' I waved back.

'I wish you could stay,' I thought, 'and help with the unicorns.'

For the first time, as I watched her retreating back (pigtails bobbing against the faded cotton), I felt lonely. I longed for another child to share the journey with me. Travelling with a great-aunt who was sometimes not quite of this world, and a herd of mythical animals, only visible at night, was all very well. But it would have been good to have had someone like myself to talk to.

7. The Horse Fair

*In which a new Enemy comes upon the
scene; is welcomed by an old one; and money
– of a sort – changes hands.*

'I have failed in my command,' stormed the Major. He was
furious with himself for having neglected to 'do his duty'. 'I
ought to have been more alert. I should have anticipated the
danger.'

'Anybody can make a mistake,' said my aunt soothingly.
'We were all tired; we had had a long night. The main thing
is to get the unicorn back as soon as possible.'

Major Fitzwilliam-Harker consulted his watch. Already, it
was three o'clock; the bidding would soon be under way. It
was decided to send Nutmouse into town to act as Scout (a
sort of Secret Agent) and that I, as the only person qualified
to lead the unicorn out of danger, should accompany him.

'Now that she has fallen into the hands of Man, only a
young girl can save her,' Aunt Emm explained. 'Thank
goodness you came with us.'

'What if she has faded at last, and I can't see her?' I felt
panic rising at the thought of so much responsibility.

'If she has, she will be beyond Human power; the danger
will have been averted,' my aunt replied. In case I should
need it, she gave me a sprig of white lavender which, she
said, would help me with 'the Sight'.

'It must be used only sparingly,' she warned. 'Frequent use
will lead to blindness.'

With the herb in my pocket, I joined Nutmouse (trilby hat
tilted over his right eye) upon the road.

'Hurry, Nutmouse! Hurry!'

The little man displayed an infuriating lack of urgency ('Some Scout!' I thought). He would keep stopping to pluck leaves from the hedge, stuffing them into his trouser pocket.

'Come *on*, Nutmouse! We're not on a nature ramble.'

To my dismay, people leading animals and cars drawing horse-boxes were beginning to pass us, coming back from the fair. I kept my eyes skinned for a black and white 'pony' with cloven feet and a short gold horn upon her head, but she was not amongst the purchases.

We reached the town at last to find the proceedings drawing to a close. Everywhere iron-clad hooves echoed upon the tarmac as horses and ponies were led away. There was much shouting and waving of sticks as frightened animals were being loaded into vans. People in holiday mood were standing round talking to their friends, and already, in the market square, the pubs and snack-bars were doing a roaring trade.

There was still a small crowd gathered round the sale-ring. Forcing my way through, I was in time to see 'Lot 105'— a roan gelding that I recognised as belonging to the travellers—being taken out. 'Lot 106' (the last), with a sticker slapped on her rump, was about to make her entry. It was our piebald unicorn!

I would have no need, I thought, for Aunt Emm's sprig of lavender; the unicorn looked as solid and real as any of the animals being loaded in the square. Was it fear that had robbed her of the ability to fade? Plainly, she was terrified. Someone had managed to get a halter round her head, and she was plunging and kicking against the rope, lashing out at the hands that urged her forward. Once in the ring she stood rooted, shuddering from crest to tail.

I glanced at the circle of faces watching her. Lined weather-beaten faces with shrewd narrow eyes; hard men! At present, each face bore a look of studied pacifity, feigning indifference. But, sooner or later, one of them would start to bid.

What use was a magic herb? I needed something more practical. 'What are we going to do? We've no money to buy her back,' I hissed to Nutmouse.

My question went unanswered. Nutmouse had pulled his hat even further over his face. He seemed lost in thought.

The bidding began. It was slow.

'There's something odd about that mare,' commented the man next to me. 'I wouldn't trust her.'

'Too delicate for me.' His friend, a dried-up stick of man, squinted at her sideways. 'Wouldn't be up to my sort of work.

And, she's deformed. Look! There's a bone sticking from her forehead.'

'The creature's mad,' said a third man, as a touch from the handler's whip sent the unicorn into a frenzy of bucks and kicks. 'Fit only for meat. You'll notice the butcher is interested.'

I took a deep breath, forcing myself to stand upright as the ring of faces swam before my eyes. I was painfully conscious of not living up to my aunt's expectations. I felt helpless, surrounded by all these men, their wallets stuffed with notes. 'Oh, Nutmouse!' I cried silently. 'Wake up! Why don't you *do* something?'

There was something unpleasantly familiar about the fat man, alluded to as the 'butcher', who was standing near the auctioneer's box. His heavy jowls, short neck and round shoulders reminded me of somebody I knew. It was hard to make out his features, for his face was shaded by a bowler hat and he wore dark glasses. Every now and then, he raised his cane (a cruel goad with a metal point) and beat against the side of the box to show that he was bidding.

The crowd of men in their tweed jackets and caps, their twill trousers, their breeches and boots, their felt hats, their quilted 'huskeys', spun like a wheel; the sounds of the market square waned and throbbed, now faint, now booming. At the hub of a reeling world, only the unicorn was firm and still.

'Only a young girl can save her. Thank goodness you are with us!' With my aunt's words singing in my ears, I raised my hand.

I thought the auctioneer might ignore my feeble signal. But he saw it, and nodded tersely. The butcher saw it, too. He turned his dark glasses (two empty black saucers) in my direction; then he lifted his goad and thumped it against the box.

Wincing, I raised my hand again.

'Don't buy her, lass,' one of the three men who were standing beside me croaked behind his hand. 'She's wicked.'

'I have just the pony for you, m'dear,' whispered another. 'Would you like to come and look at her?'

I took no notice. Staring fixedly at the auctioneer, I went on bidding. He looked uncomfortable; his eyes were shifty. I judged, from the glances being exchanged between him and the butcher that they had some sort of agreement. I gritted my teeth, holding up my hand.

Other interest in the mare was fading. One by one, the few opposing bidders were dropping out. It was left to me and the butcher. My hand felt sticky; tingles were running up and down my back. The butcher, I could see, was going purple in the face. The exchange of glances with the auctioneer had ceased. Greed had overtaken the salesman; he was intent only on forcing up the price.

It was going too high! I could feel waves of disapproval passing amongst the seasoned horsemen in the crowd. The 'dried stick', who had rejected the mare earlier, tugged at my sleeve.

'Stop it, lass. Are you mad? She isn't worth it. Be a good girl, now. Go home to your mammy,' he pleaded.

'You can have my pony for half the price,' persisted his friend.

'I don't want your pony. I want this one.' Tears stung my eyes.

'It's against you, dear.' The auctioneer looked at me, sharply. Then, someone else joined in the bidding.

I could not see who it was. He was a short man, hidden by the crowd. All I could see was a black bowler hat, bobbing up like a football each time he lifted it.

'It's hopeless, Nutmouse. Aunt Emm couldn't afford the price.' In despair, I turned to my companion. I realised with a shock that he was gone. I had been deserted.

'Your bid?' Eyebrows raised, the auctioneer nodded in my direction. 'Your bid, I say.' Numbly, I shook my head. ('She's a little chestnut,' the pony-owner whispered in my ear. 'And can she jump!' I did not answer.)

There seemed little point in my staying; yet, somehow, I had to be there at the end. I stood, transfixed, listening to the auctioneer's voice droning on, the butcher's metal-tipped goad tapping in counterpoint against the box. The opposing bidder was making him look foolish. 'The price of beef will be going up,' somebody mocked. There was general laughter. The butcher's face turned from purple to almost black; he smashed his cane against the box, in fury.

It was all over. Through a haze, I could see the handler dragging the unicorn from the ring. In my confused state of mind, I could not tell who had bought her. I had a sudden mad idea of approaching the auctioneer to tell him the whole story (the part he would believe, anyway), to explain that the sale had been a mistake; the mare was ours. My feet would not move.

Somebody nudged my elbow. Thinking it was the seller of the chestnut pony, I was about to snap my answer when, glancing down, I saw his hand.

There was no mistaking it! Nor, for that matter, was there any mistaking the ginger whiskers protruding from beneath the brim of a black bowler, as the little man brushed past me on his way to the auctioneer's stand.

He had been wearing a trilby. Wasn't that good enough for the purpose? Where does he get his hats from anyway? The air? Disappointment and fear exploded into anger. 'Why did you bid against me?' I wanted to shout at him. 'When you knew we hadn't the money.'

Nutmouse pushed his bowler to the back of his head. He was looking smug as he dug into his trouser pocket and produced—not leaves from the hedgerow—but a whole sheaf of crisp new banknotes! He handed the money to the auctioneer's clerk and, in exchange, received the rope. Winking, he signalled to me to follow.

With a roar like an angry bull, the butcher took a step as if to stop us. He was prevented by the auctioneer laying a warning hand upon his shoulder. We left them arguing vociferously as we picked our way across the emptying square, taking the road towards our camp.

'What will happen when the money turns back into leaves?' I asked Nutmouse, when I had forgiven him sufficiently to speak.

He shrugged, fluttering his fingers in a manner that suggested foliage falling in the autumn. Apparently the outcome did not concern him.

'Well, at least Maggie's Uncle Jack won't make anything out of it,' I thought. 'Serves him right. And that auctioneer, too. I'm sure he was in league with the butcher.'

I took over the leading of the unicorn. She seemed reluctant to follow anybody but me, pressing her body against mine as we walked. She felt cold; now and again she shivered violently. I contemplated taking off my cardigan and laying it across her back, but decided that such human contact would only harm her further. 'I will remove the halter as soon as I can,' I whispered, knowing that it was hurting her. 'Just wait till we get away from the people.' In the meantime, I concentrated on trying to look like a normal girl who had just bought a new pony, walking home. The presence of Nutmouse at my side did not help the image, I suspected.

At the edge of the town, we halted. Nutmouse plucked the number '106' from the unicorn's rump, slapped it on his hat and tossed them both to the top of the nearest lamp-post. Laughing, I unfastened the halter, setting the unicorn free to follow. I watched with relief as she began to fade, at last . . . Then Nutmouse and I clasped hands, dancing a jig of triumph.

One thing, however, spoilt the pleasure of our achievement. We were just drawing level with an isolated pub on the outskirts when a van drove by, pulling in and halting on the forecourt. The driver of the van got out, slamming the door and taking off his dark glasses as he was greeted by a friend. It did not need the writing on the side of the van to tell me, then, who the butcher was. Without his glasses, and with his hat raised in greeting, he was so like the newsvendor as to be mistaken for his double.

The name upon the van was Behan.

Charles Henry Oliver Patrick BEHAN
FAMILY BUTCHER.
Freezer Service—Prime Steak a Speciality.

Charles Henry Oliver Patrick—CHOP! His friend I knew. It was Mr. Potts!

8. The Dreaming Daisies

*In which a field of moon-daisies becomes
an almost fatal attraction; and the travellers
are attacked by Enemy forces.*

My aunt received the news with some alarm.

'I knew he would come after us,' she said, 'but I had hoped
the villagers of Glencoppaleen might hold him at bay a little
longer. I was not expecting him so soon.'

'Full alert! Emergency plans!' ordered the Major. Without
waiting for sunset, we struck camp.

We marched for five nights on what the Major called 'iron
rations'—a snatched sandwich or a hastily opened tin—
stopping only for brief periods at a time, and sleeping,
whenever we could, in the shadow of a 'fairy fort'. Such
places, said my aunt, offered protection from all danger. She
did something mysterious with an ash-wand round the
circumference of each ancient mound before we unloaded.

The unicorns became weary. *And* footsore. Nutmouse was
obliged to don his farrier's cap and apron and change their
shoes. The poor mare I had rescued from the fair lagged
behind the others. I noticed that she was growing thin, and
her knowledge of when to fade and when to reappear was
becoming more and more confused. Sometimes she blinked
on and off like a light signal.

'It was that halter,' deplored my aunt. 'The rope has
burned into her very being. Only a chain of daisies may be
used to lead a unicorn.' Feverishly she rubbed the creature's
head and neck with every lotion in her medicine-chest.
Camomile, feverfew, rose-water, a cocoction of self-heal and

woundwort; they all provided some relief, but it was fleeting.

We saw no one, though we were bothered by birds. If we left the shelter of a fort before moonrise or after moonset, evil-looking magpies and rooks would bombard us with sticks and stones.

'The butcher's cohorts,' snorted the Major. 'A rag-bag army! No discipline.' He reached into his gun-holster for some bull's-eyes to shoot at them. The attackers retreated to the tree-tops, cawing and cackling their defiance. Next day, they returned in greater numbers.

Halfway across County Meath, the unicorns became rebellious. They clustered together, showing white edges at the rims of their usually gentle eyes, clashing horns, snapping and squealing at each other, irritably. The strain of the journey was beginning to show. If they did not get a proper rest soon, we would have a mutiny on our hands.

I was leading, for the Major, after some argument, had accepted my aunt's offer of a lift. Nutmouse was trotting at my side, carrying the compass. How many times, I wondered, had we reason to be grateful for the Weaver's gift, as the compass veered this way and that; now pointing us to a safer pass; now indicating a quieter, more secret route? At present, the tiny horse was still, fixed like a figure-head at the front of a vessel. Its red eyes glinted in the light of a moon that was past its full, but still bright enough to show miles of road stretching ahead.

All of a sudden Nutmouse stopped, wheeling round with a grunt.

The unicorns had broken off their petty quarrelling. They had come to a halt, all crowded in an open gateway. Ears pricked, nostrils flaring, they were staring into a field.

'What's up with them, now?' I played their favourite bird song on the flute. There was no response. In the silence that followed, I could hear the night breeze buffeting the hedges. Some way away an owl screeched; it was like a warning.

By this time my aunt's car had drawn up, and the Major got out to have a look.

'Moon-daisies!' he informed us. 'A whole field of 'em.'

'We'll never get them past those,' groaned Aunt Emm, 'After orchids and wild thyme, they are their favourite flowers.' Indeed, the field did look very beautiful in the

moonlight, with the big white daisies shimmering and nodding in the breeze. Large fur-coated moths with jewel-like eyes were blundering heavily from flower to flower. The stallion stamped his foot and whinnied urgently. 'All right,' said my aunt. 'You may go in.'

We spread a rug upon the ground, and Aunt Emm went

into the caravan to make tea and cut some sandwiches. It was a relief, after all those nights of hasty travel, to lie back in the lea of the hedge and watch the unicorns rolling and sporting in the daisies. Weariness forgotten, for the first time since leaving the peaceful valley of Glencoppaleen they took to the air. Scattering the moths they skimmed, long manes and tails streaming behind them, two inches above the moonlit flowers. Eventually they landed, softly as snowflakes, to bury their noses in white blooms and set about the serious business of eating. Replete with tomato sandwiches and hot sweet tea, I yawned, half-closing my eyes.

'Do we have to go on to Inishnallis?' I asked sleepily. 'Wouldn't this do? Couldn't we just stay here?'

'It is very pleasant, but it would not last.' My aunt's voice sounded muffled and far-away.

The first indication that something was wrong was when the foal keeled over and lay flat upon his side. We thought that he was merely snatching a quick nap, as small foals do. Presently, however, his mother gave a shudder and lay down beside him. Fighting off a drowsiness that had been creeping up ever since I sat beneath the hedge, I looked around.

Everywhere, unicorns were drooping and sinking like fading flowers. Their knees were bending, their gold horns dipping low, their long white manes spreading out across the ground. The whole herd was rolling into the daisies and falling asleep! Trip, who had tired of chasing moths and was patting at a flower, gave a sudden squeal as if he had been stung and licked his paw. He, too, crumpled up, closing his eyes.

'They're drugged! The daisies are drugged. And I know who did it!'

'The Enemy have out-flanked us,' cried the Major.

My aunt snatched up the cat, shaking him, breathing into his nose, forcing him awake. 'Get the unicorns out of the field before it is too late,' she shouted.

'How?' I sprang up, playing my flute for all I was worth. The Major dashed to the caravan and, grabbing the bugle, sounded 'Reveille'.

Not a unicorn stirred. The moths lumbered carelessly among the flowers. Nutmouse ran in and out amongst the herd, clapping his hands and poking the sleeping animals in the ribs. When this had no effect, he fell to plucking the daisies—blowing on each bloom—and bringing me great armfuls.

'What's the fellow doing?' snapped the Major, sneezing and spluttering as the white powder Nutmouse had blown from the flowers went up his nose. 'Has he gone off his head?'

'Very much *on* it, I should say,' replied my aunt, producing her silk handkerchief and waving the powder away. 'Mind Tripitaka.' She thrust the drowsy cat into his arms. 'Jennifer! To work!'

'Only a chain of daisies may be used to lead a unicorn!' I saw her purpose.

'But,' I objected, backing away from the mounting pile of flowers that Nutmouse was laying at my feet, 'you said the daisies were drugged.'

'So they are. And, knowing Mr. Potts, the drug he used will have been potent. We must take precautionary measures straight away. Leaves of wake-robin—the wild arum—you'll find them growing behind the hedge. Gather as many as you can. Quickly! I'll reboil the kettle.'

It took five minutes for the antidote to brew. 'It should have been seven—the magic number,' said my aunt. 'But we can wait no longer.' She put a little on a handkerchief to help the Major who, cat in arms, was swaying backwards and forwards, struggling to keep his eyes open.

We searched for a watering-can, but could not find one. Nutmouse, who seemed immune to the effects of the drug ('That is because he is older than any of us,' said my aunt, somewhat mysteriously), lent us his blacksmith's bellows.

With a small hole in the leather, into which we poured the
liquid, it made a splendid spray. When the daisies had been
well-soaked I began, hands trembling, to split a stem and
insert a bloom, linking flower to flower. My aunt sat down
on the grass to help. In no time, nine pale garlands were
strewn at our feet. Picking up the longest, I approached the
stallion. He was not quite asleep. His beautiful dark eyes were
partly open; but they were misting over.

'Come on, boy,' I urged. I wound the garland round his
neck, and pulled. He sighed. His ears flicked, feebly. He
resisted.

Digging my feet into the ground, I tugged again. 'The
stalks will snap,' I thought.

But they didn't! Gradually, stumbling and slipping, the
stallion staggered to his feet. I coaxed him to the road and,
leaving him in the care of Nutmouse and my aunt, hurried
back for the mare and foal.

One by one, I brought them out. The big piebald mare was the hardest to rouse. It took a fresh infusion of wakerobin leaves to get her to stir at all. Then Nutmouse was obliged to stand beside her, pinching her to keep her awake.

By the time all the unicorns, heads low, eyelids drooping, were standing on the road dawn was approaching. The sky was growing opalescent, like the inside of a shell.

'Walk on! Walk on! The only cure is movement. *Quick* march, Major, if you please.' My aunt's hair haloed her head, wilder than usual, as she hurried to start the car.

With a supreme effort, the cavalcade resumed its journey. Drawing all the breath I could manage into my lungs, I put the flute to my lips. The sounds that came out were faint and dreary, the plaintive notes of marsh-birds, heard a long way off. Nutmouse gave me a scornful look and commenced to whistle.

The unicorns staggered forward. Their hunched forms pulsed—now there, now gone—as elusive as sunbeams on a cloudy day. Just as I thought they were beginning to revive, the Major put his field-glass to his eye.

'Storm-clouds, following,' he reported. 'Take cover.'

About half a mile along the road was the dark outline of a pinewood. Putting our heads down, we began to run. The clouds came over fast. They were not rain-clouds as we supposed, but flock upon flock of big black birds.

'The butcher's hooded-crows,' cried Aunt Emm from the car. 'His crack forces! Jennifer! Nutmouse! Get the unicorns into the wood, while we try to divert them.'

The 'Charge' rang out upon the bugle. I waited long enough to see the Major produce a large umbrella, unfurling it and waving it to and fro (the silk handkerchief was fluttering from the car window, my aunt was bleeping on the horn). Then I took to my heels and ran after Nutmouse.

Borne by a surge of unseen movement, as the unicorns (now completely invisible) galloped with us, we tore towards the wood. Their hooves pattered like hail upon the road. Trees loomed in front of us. 'We're safe!' I thought—just as the first crow detached himself from the flock and flew straight at us.

He must have dug his talons into the mare beside me, for I heard her scream. I was so angry that I attacked him with my fists, beating him over and over with my bare hands. He left the mare and came at me with a squawk. I was aware of searing pain, of blood gushing down my cheek as I went down, blinded and half-suffocated in a mass of fetid plumage.

Somewhere beyond my heaving stinking aggressor, I heard a sharp ping, a whine. A stone caught him on the side, sending him tumbling. But by now he was not alone. Crow upon crow came dropping from the sky in a dark snow-storm of black and grey feathers. Nutmouse, working hard with the catapult he had taken from his pocket, was overpowered. He fell to his knees beneath a cape of fluttering wings and squawking bodies.

Then, an amazing thing occurred. The little man managed to free one hand. Shaking his attackers off his head, he put two fingers in his mouth and whistled.

'Am I dreaming?' I wondered. For, as the shrill sound died I thought I heard the sound of the Weaver's loom—'Whoosh-and-clonk! Whoosh-and-clonk!'

Up from the south-east, there came a gale-force wind. It roared along the road like a beast of prey, cracking branches, tossing hedgerows like demented animals. Gates were flattened in its wake. My aunt's car rocked. It caught the Major's umbrella and sent it spinning into the air. The unicorns were engulfed like a wave, and Nutmouse and I were blown aside into the haven of the wood . . . .

And it carried away the crows, like so many flapping, protesting tatters of black rag.

9. The Gamekeeper

*In which the Company find themselves in
the line of fire; Squew-wiff runs into trouble; and
the herd experiences a tragic loss.*

It was very dark in the wood. And eerie. The tail-end of the
wind mourned like a *banshee* though the branches above our
heads. Aunt Emm had to use her headlights as she drove the
car, squelching and skidding, along a loggers' trail. I was
thankful for the Weaver's compass, glowing like a lighted
taper in the blackness and beckoning me onward through the
tall trunks of the trees. When we judged we were safely at
the centre, we stopped and set up camp.

'All present and correct,' announced the Major, after he
had counted the unicorns. My aunt brought out the sticking-
plaster and bandages and attended to the wounded.

'None of them is badly hurt,' she reported. 'Thanks to the
prompt action of the Weaver.'

'I'm going to recommend you for promotion,' the Major
told Nutmouse. 'Valour and quick thinking in the heat of
battle.' The object of his admiration donned a lieutenant's
beret, and saluted smartly.

We passed an uncomfortable day. The unicorns were
restless. We could hear them scuffling in the fallen pine-
needles beyond the caravan wall. Squiff complained loudly
and constantly because there was nothing to eat but turnip.
The wound on my cheek throbbed beneath its poultice of
sphagnum moss, and had to be re-dressed.

When the wind had dropped, it started to rain. Water
forced its way through the pine-needle canopy, pattering on

the roof and keeping us awake. When it stopped, the birds returned. Not the loathsome crows, but the magpies and rooks that had bothered us before. My aunt and I huddled together, while leftover raindrops pinged into a bucket from a leak in the roof, and listened to their croaking.

'They are spies,' said Aunt Emm grimly. 'Reporting to "Headquarters" I shouldn't be surprised.'

At nightfall (apparent only by an increased blackness in which the unicorns floated like pearly ghosts) the birds flew away. After a scrappy meal, we pressed on through the wood.

It took most of the night to reach the far side. Here, the evergreens were replaced by a broad belt of oak, with now and again a clump of elder. Tall bracken made the going difficult even on a cart-track, and more than once the car engine stalled.

'It's almost daybreak,' said the Major, setting his shoulder to the caravan during one of these stops and giving it a push. 'We might as well call a halt.'

We kept well within the shadow of the oaks, for a large house could be glimpsed across a park and, as my aunt said, we could not be sure of our reception. Once again, the unicorns were fretful. They wheeled about, turning their tails towards the wind and puffing through their nostrils at the penetrating carrion-smell of the elder flowers.

> *Old woman, old woman,*
> *Come not near me*

my aunt recited, waving her ash-wand. The elder, she explained, was a tree much beloved of black witches.

'We should not have camped near them,' she said to the Major. 'They will bring us ill fortune.'

'We had little choice.' The Major had fallen into one of his glooms. 'Anyhow,' he brightened, 'silly old hags on broomsticks don't scare me. They're just a lot of show-offs, with their crook-backs and cackles. No,' he gulped down his tea, dabbing his moustache with his spotless white handkerchief, 'it's those birds that bother me. If they come back today, I'll shoot them. No bull's-eyes. Live amunition!'

'Dear Major,' smiled my aunt, passing him the toast. 'Even if you had some, you wouldn't use it. You're much too soft-hearted.'

In the event, it was not the Major who shot at the birds. When breakfast was over, I left the others to do the washing-up and took Squew-wiff in his pen to the borders of the park. My nerves, I decided, would not stand another day of his demands for better fare than turnip.

The wound upon my cheek had ceased to throb. I removed the sphagnum moss, placing it in a damp shady hollow where I hoped it might grow. The sun was rising, promising a lovely day. I wasted some time watching the brilliant colours flooding like spilt paint-water across the sky. Rabbits were out for their morning forage in the short grass of the park—

whole families of them, ranging from fat prosperous bucks down to tiny 'bunnies' like clockwork toys. Squiff, feeling lonesome, lifted his nose, uttering guinea-pig shouts for their attention. Completely self-sufficient they ignored his overtures, carrying on with their routine. Nibble and bob; nibble and bob. Disheartened, he subsided into silence and followed their example.

I was on the point of turning back towards the camp when I saw them coming. First one black dot, then another, then another; polluting the clear orange of the dawn. Raising his ears, a buck thumped a warning with his hind foot on the ground, and the rabbits disappeared in a flurry of white tails. Small birds that had been carolling their delight in a new day, laying claim to territories within the wood, fell silent as, one by one, the intruders landed heavily upon the branches.

They were not allowed to rest for long. Scarcely had they opened their bills to utter the first croak, than a shot rang out. Sharp as a whipcrack! One of the marauders, a large magpie with a broken feather in his tail, dropped like a stone. His companions did not wait to find out what hit him. With raucous clamour, they arose from the trees and fled.

'Whatever next?' I thought.

But as I started to run towards the camp, I was engulfed by the unicorns (mist-like—evaporating) swirling past me, as they stampeded in the opposite direction. I gave no thought to the hidden gunman; no consideration to the consequences of our being discovered.

'AUNT EMM! MAJOR! NUTMOUSE!' I yelled with the full force of my lungs. 'Come *quick*! The unicorns are running away.'

It took all morning for Aunt Emm and the Major to round them up from the park. I was of little use; only able to pick out the odd unicorn through the Major's telescope. Nutmouse did not offer his assistance. At the sound of the shot he had vanished, later to be found hiding in a tree. 'He will face the blackest sorcery; but cold lead is a different matter,' my aunt said, with understanding.

On closer inspection, the blinds were found to be drawn on the windows of the house. The owner was away; there was no likelihood of our being observed from that quarter. In our anxiety about the unicorns we had overlooked the fact that the gunman, whoever he was, might still be lurking, but when the last member of the herd, trembling and snorting (I could not see her, but I could *feel* her fear), was gathered with the others in the shelter of the trees, my aunt announced, 'We cannot stay here. It is far too dangerous. Jennifer! Go and fetch that guinea-pig of yours, and we'll be off.'

I ran to do her bidding. When I reached the spot where I had left him, I found to my horror that the pen had been smashed and overturned; Squiff was nowhere to be found!

For once, the Major was unsympathetic. 'I have no use for deserters,' he told me. 'The army will have to march without him.'

'I'm not leaving without Squiff. I'm going to look for him.' It was open rebellion.

'Take Tripitaka. He will be of use, I think,' Aunt Emm said briskly. 'Meanwhile, we will pack up. You can follow when you've found him.'

Brown tail carried like a banner, Tripitaka picked his way fastidiously across the damp grass of the park. Now and then, a bird would claim his attention, or he would pause to sniff a flower. 'He imagines himself to be on one of his "walks",' I thought sourly.

Nevertheless he went on unerringly, straight to a place where the woodland protruded like a long tongue into the park. Here, beneath a large elm, there was a hut; before the hut, a fence. With revulsion, I noticed shrivelled corpses of those animals that gamekeepers call 'vermin' hanging on the wires. Of these, the body of the broken-tailed magpie was the freshest and the largest.

Trip stopped so abruptly that I cannoned into him, and he rebuked me with a yowl. Gazing sadly up at me from the rank grass beneath the fence was my guinea-pig.

He was still alive! I could not understand why he made no attempt to move—until I saw the fine piece of wire running towards the peg, half-buried in the ground. Down on my knees, I probed with my fingers and Squiff gave a squeal; his hind-leg was caught tightly in a noose.

Cradling the little animal on my knees, I worked with caution to free him from the snare. One clumsy move, I knew, could frighten him into a heart-attack, or cause him to struggle and break his leg. Even after I had loosened the cruel loop, I sat there stroking him and talking to him quietly. The wire had cut into his leg, leaving it raw and swollen. Otherwise, he was unharmed. He had been lucky! When I was sure that he was calm, I placed him in my pocket and rose to go.

As I got to my feet, I looked up. And found myself staring into the hard eyes of a man.

For a moment, neither of us moved. His eyes, I noted, were slate-grey. Almost black. His hair, flopping over his forehead, was dark brown. He carried a shot-gun resting in the crook of his arm. There was a sharp 'click' as he closed the barrel.

'You're trespassing,' he said at last. 'Didn't you see the notice?'

'No,' I answered. 'We came in through the wood.' A wave of anger surged through me. 'You've hurt my guinea-pig,' I told him. 'He was caught in one of your traps.'

The man shrugged. 'You'd best be going,' was all he said.

I prepared to leave—when a sudden rustling in the wood nearby delayed me. The unicorn foal was standing on the far side of the fence, watching us.

I suppose he must have followed me. During the journey we had grown very close, and often, in that time between the fading of the moon and sunrise, we had played together.

I do not know what Power made me see him then, just that last time, with the sunlight dappling through the leaves on to his jet-black coat, and catching his tiny horn so that it twinkled like a star. I am certain the gamekeeper did not see him at all; he only heard a noise. He must have thought it was a fox. He raised his gun, and shot in that direction!

What followed was like a nightmare. The foal folded up and dropped silently, like a cast-off piece of clothing. I was vaguely aware of Trip's angry snarl as he sprang towards the man, the gamekeeper's oath as he shook him off. I think he said something about 'damaging his covers', as he strode away ....

I crawled through the fence to be beside the foal. With one hand on Squiff's warm fur for comfort, I watched his body fade, melting to a shadow. I felt dry and desolate; no tears would come.

'Why did it happen?' I demanded of my aunt when, summoned by Trip, she hastened to my side, 'Why ... why ... *why*?' But, deep inside, I thought I knew.

'If ...,' I cried. I could get no further; the tears were flooding.

'Come away,' my aunt said gently. 'I have something to show you.' She led me to where the Major was waiting with Nutmouse and the rest of the herd. 'Over here,' she called softly. In my numbed state, I supposed her to be talking to me—until I felt warm breath against my cheek.

'It's the stallion,' said Aunt Emm. With her hand on mine, she guided my fingers towards him. 'What do you feel?'

'His horn,' I said.

'What else?' Her hand tightened on mine. I could sense the stallion bowing his head as if in submission, as I ran my fingers along the horn.

'There is a ridge,' I said. 'A deep line. Going round and round.'

'Precisely!' My aunt was triumphant. 'That is the message

of the unicorn's horn. It stands for the Eternal Spiral—birth, death, rebirth—going round and round.'

I stopped crying. It seemed too much to take in, but her words gave comfort.

My hand had come to the end of the stallion's horn. 'It comes to a point,' I reminded her. 'Beyond that is . . .'

'Air—the breath of Life,' said my aunt, 'containing the gases we need for our existence, and carrying dust-specks, water-droplets, pollen. The very fabric of New Beginnings.'

'But . . . ,' I argued.

'I prefer the word you used earlier,' Aunt Emm remarked. 'If! It's a shorter word, but as long as my arm. Full of possibilities.'

She handed me her silk handkerchief. As I wiped my eyes, I noticed a small blue butterfly, like a fragment of the sky, fluttering towards us. It settled. Apparently in mid-air.

But I knew, from the soft snuffling sounds, that it was poised on the stallion's nose.

10. Gertrude Speede

In which the Enemy has some success;
speed becomes essential; and transmogrification
is the order of the day.

It was a sad little band that left the shade of the great oak in the centre of the park where we had buried the foal (a place where rabbits tunnelled beneath the roots of the old tree and the thrush sang its twice-repeated song of hope from the topmost branches). With heavy hearts, we returned to the road.

The mother of the foal kept looking back and calling. Eventually, when no answer came, she sighed; a great shuddering sigh, as if her grief was too hard to hold. After this she seemed resigned. But her eyes, I noticed, were dull, and she kept close to the stallion for support. The other unicorns dragged their feet, plodding, ears flopping like mules. In the dim light of a waning moon their horns looked tarnished.

'Morale in the ranks is very low,' deplored the Major.

'They miss the foal,' said Aunt Emm. 'So few of them are born these days. Come now, Jennifer!' She pushed back her hair, straightening her shoulders. 'This won't do. Play us some bird song on the flute to take us forward. The storm-cock, brave in the face of wind and rain, would be apt, I think.'

'Aunt Emm,' I hardly dared to speak, 'I haven't got it... the flute, I mean. I must have dropped it when...'

Aunt Emm's shoulders sagged once more. For the first time on the journey she looked close to despair. 'There will be triple misfortune,' she murmured, her fingers playing nervously with one of her carbuncle rings. 'Troubles always come in threes. Well, we can't go back; we'll have to manage without it . . . Nutmouse!' she commanded, 'whistle, please.'

'Troubles come in threes,' my aunt had said. Fate was about to prove her theory correct.

With the darkening of the moon, at that time when the nights are black, we had our second loss. The big piebald mare who, since her kidnap and rescue from the fair, had been growing fainter and fainter until I could hardly make her out at all, vanished one night. She did not return.

'She is pure spirit, now,' Aunt Emm told me. 'Poor thing! Her fight between reality and dreams has been a long one. I thought the Earth would claim her and she would belong to men, but she has chosen the Air. She will join the winds. The Weaver will look after her.'

'Will he look after the foal?' I asked bitterly.

'He, or Someone greater,' replied my aunt.

We plodded forward through the dark nights with only the car headlights and the Weaver's compass to light our path. I began to wonder if we had been right to take the unicorns from their peaceful valley, forcing such rare and fragile creatures to undertake so hazardous a journey. When I voiced my thoughts to my aunt, however, she shook her head.

'Soon there will be no valley left,' she reminded me. 'Just a sheet of empty water, tamed and harnessed for the use of men. Besides the Enemy had discovered the unicorns' whereabouts. Would you have us leave the herd to *their* tender mercy?'

'But the Enemy still know where they are. They're following us,' I persisted.

'That may be so,' my aunt answered crisply. 'But please don't underestimate the Major's ability to lead us, or Nutmouse's skills. Or, for that matter, your own usefulness. Besides, have you not noticed—we have friends?'

I began to see that she was right. As the summer breezes whispered in the darkened hedgerows, teasing out the scents of wild rose and honeysuckle, still warm and aromatic from the evening sun, I became conscious of a big bird flying on muffled wings in front of us. In the daytime, his place was taken by a starling; a gaudy show-off who stood guard on a tree, post, gate (anything convenient to our camp) and entertained us with his repertoire of the songs of other birds. It was noticeable that the magpies and rooks were absent.

The rising of a new moon went some way towards restoring the unicorns' spirits. As its silver crescent swelled, they managed a slow trot.

'Morale is improving,' declared the Major. He ordered an extra supply of wild thyme and orchids all round.

We were camped on the shores of Lough Sheelin. It had been a beautiful day with blue sky overhead and sunlight dancing on the sparkling water. Despite the fact that a strict watch had been kept, there had been no sighting of the enemy since we left the wood. We were in buoyant mood. Evening was drawing in and the unicorns were reappearing in ones and twos, browsing contentedly on white puffs of bog-cotton in the marsh.

All at once, Nutmouse looked up from his supper and gave a grunt. 'Listen!' said my aunt.

Down on the road, somebody was playing the flute!

I don't know why, but my immediate conclusion was that it was the Weaver. I sprang to my feet. The unicorns had heard it, too. Their heads were raised; one of them whinnied. In single file, they left the marsh and trouped towards the road.

'Come back, come back!' chirped the starling, fluttering anxiously from the caravan roof to a nearby willow and back again. The unicorns took no notice. He uttered a low sound like 'Fools!' and flew off in a huff.

We followed the unicorns as if enchanted. But at the verge the Major uttered a low 'Cave', and drew us back behind a wall.

A large cattle-truck was parked upon the road. The driver was lounging in the cab, his fat elbow protruding through the window as he blew a cloud of smoke from his cigar. The bowler hat was pushed back, rakishly, upon his head; despite the fact that it was growing late, he still wore dark glasses. 'Chop Behan . . . the butcher!' I nudged my aunt. She nodded.

At the back of the truck the ramp was down, and we could see Mr. Potts squatting in an ungainly fashion in the straw. He was swaying from side to side like an Indian snake-charmer. With pale cheeks swollen as if from toothache, he puffed for all he was worth upon the Weaver's flute.

'Con-men! Robbers!' growled the Major. We watched, helpless, as the unicorns streamed up the ramp into the box.

One final, discordant note, and Mr. Potts leapt down. 'Give us a hand,' he shouted to the butcher irritably. Together, they raised the ramp. Chains rattled; the bolts shot home.

The unicorns stamped and neighed—Too late!

The chemist and his accomplice sprang into the cab. The engine choked, then rumbled. The truck bore its stolen cargo away, to be swallowed gradually by the gathering gloom.

We sprang to life. 'After them!' roared the Major.

We all piled into the car; the Major in the passenger-seat, Nutmouse (with Trip on his knee) and me behind. My aunt put her foot down and we were off.

The cattle-truck could still be seen in the distance, heading south.

'Charge!' cried the Major, waving his swagger-stick. 'The Company of the Hare to the rescue.' My aunt stamped on the accelerator, and the old car rattled in pursuit.

We were gaining! Then there came a sudden cough—a splutter. We lost power. 'We've run out of petrol,' despaired Aunt Emm, as the car taxied to a stop.

'Where's the nearest petrol-station?'

'Miles back!'

'Will it still be open at this hour?'

'They'll be half-way to Dublin by now,' lamented the Major. 'Machinery! I never could abide it.' He gave the car a kick.

'There is no call to lose your temper, Toby,' said my aunt severely. 'What is it, Nutmouse?' This to the little man who was tugging at her sleeve and grunting feverishly.

'What's the fellow saying?' demanded the Major. 'I can't understand him when he speaks so fast.'

'He's reminding me of a friend of ours,' my aunt told him. 'Gertrude Speede lives quite close by. We'll ask her for assistance.'

'*Not* Gertie Speede!' the Major groaned. 'I can't stand women drivers!' He blushed, glancing at my aunt. 'Present company excepted,' he added hastily.

We abandoned our car by the side of the road, and retraced our tracks. About a quarter of a mile from where we had halted, we came upon a rough driveway. A sign in an old car-tyre read:

SPEEDEY BODY REPAIRS.
SPRAYING & VARNISHING.

We went up the drive and found ourselves in a yard at the back of a big house. You could hardly *see* the house for the pieces of old motor-cars piled everywhere.

'Scrap-yard! Litter-louse!' The Major's moustache rippled with distaste.

My aunt ignored him. She marched defiantly up to the back door and knocked. There was no reply. She had raised her hand to knock for a second time, when a voice came from underneath the bonnet of a nearby car.

'If it's *me* you're wanting, Emmeline Goodharte, you'd best be looking in *my* direction!'

The figure which emerged from beneath the bonnet was short and stout. It had a round, sunnily-smiling face (at least what could be seen of it behind a coating of black oil) and short, straight hair cut in a fringe that was meant to be combed across the forehead but was sticking out in spikes in all directions, indicating that the owner repeatedly ran her fingers through it when contemplating a problem. Wiping these fingers (which were coated in axle-grease) on her overalls, she advanced, hand held out, towards the Major.

'Major, me old Banger! How are you? It's light-years since we met... and Emmeline, too! It's a long while since you took my road. And who's this new model?'

She took my hand in hers. It was still greasy, but the clasp was warm and friendly. Her hazel eyes twinkled with mischief. I liked her a lot.

'Himself, of course, I know.' She nodded towards Nutmouse.

'Gertrude, we're in trouble,' said my aunt. 'I suppose you've heard the reason for our journey?'

Miss Speede nodded. 'Nuts and bolts,' she said wisely. 'Pipes and gaskets. Every part of the engine has its place and is of service to the others. What use is the clutch without the cable? Why put the petrol in the radiator? Do they not know that unicorns are part of the system too?'

'Talking of petrol,' interrupted the Major, who had been listening to all these seemingly irrelevant remarks with some impatience. 'Have you got any?'

'I have,' replied Miss Speede. 'Have you a car to put it in?'

She listened gravely to our problems, and shook her head. 'You'll want all the horse-power you can get,' she stated. 'You'd best leave your old tin in the ditch. I'll drive you.'

'Never!' The Major regarded the vehicle to which she propelled us with alarm. A glossy streamlined convertible, of a make unknown to me, it had an extremely long bonnet on which was mounted, I noted with interest, a silver mascot in the shape of a running hare.

'If you're chicken, you can stay behind,' Miss Speede told the Major. She stripped off her oily overalls, replacing them with a boiler-suit of spotless white. An orange helmet and a pair of black leather gloves completed her attire. 'You can use the time to fill up the abandoned crock. You'll find a can of petrol in the shed... Come, Emmeline. And you two! Bring the cat; he may be useful.'

So saying, she leapt lightly into the driver's seat, and fastened the safety-belt. Scarcely waiting for us to scramble aboard, she pressed one of the many buttons ranged along the glittering dashboard. The car purred into action. It did not run along the ground. We leapt the yard and driveway as if taking Becher's Brook, landing as gracefully as a falling leaf upon the highway. Miss Speede pressed a second button, and we roared past Aunt Emm's car at a hundred miles an hour.

'Steady, Gertie,' gasped my aunt. 'There's a town ahead—and lights! They're red!' She covered her eyes with her silk handkerchief.

'Bother!' said Miss Speede. She slammed her foot upon the brake, screeching to a halt. But not for long!

The lights remained steadfastly red. Then a home-going tractor rumbled across in front of us. 'I can't be bothered with this,' declared Miss Speede. She pressed another button. With stomachs sunk into our toes, we found ourselves in a small bi-plane, flying above the roofs.

Once clear of the town, the car resumed its former shape. We tore down the highway with the wind streaming in our hair.

'There's a junction ahead . . . which way . . . which way?'

'How should I know?' snapped my aunt (it was plain her nerves were rattled). 'They both go south.'

'Then, upwards would be best,' decided Miss Speede. The car became a helicopter in which we scoured the country.

'There they are! Look! Down there!' I cried.

'They're going at a good rate,' said my aunt. 'How do we stop them?'

'Easy!' Miss Speede pointed to a minor road crossing the highway. 'We'll intercept them there.'

'NO—GERTRUDE—NO!!'

Aunt Emm's cries of protest were drowned by the screaming of a motor-cycle engine as, Miss Speede bent low over the handle-bars, my aunt riding pillion, and Nutmouse, Trip and I stuffed into the bouncing sidecar, we negotiated the bends of the narrow roadway, keeling sideways, first one way, then the other.

I could see the high road slipping towards us like a dream—The sign saying 'HALT' was looming up—I could see the lights of the approaching cattle-truck cutting a slice in the road—Then there was an almighty CRASH!!!

It was all over! The lights went out; the motor-cycle muttered to a stop on the far side of the crossing.

Miss Speede produced a torch, and directed its beam towards the cattle-truck, which was perched at an odd angle upon the centre barrier, fumes spurting from beneath its bonnet. 'Chop' Behan, blood streaming from his nose and dark glasses splintered, was scrambling dazedly from his twisted cab. All that could be seen of Mr. Potts was a pair of pin-striped trousers kicking wildly in the hedge.

The occupants of the box were worryingly quiet.

'You'd best get them out while they're still in shock,' Miss Speede whispered. 'It would be easier.'

I looked at her, open-mouthed. This time it was not only her car which had changed. Miss Speede had become an elderly Jubilee nurse, trim and efficient in smart uniform with hat and bag. An ordinary push-bike with the back wheel buckled lay at her feet. She turned to accost the bewildered butcher.

'How DARE you drive so dangerously,' she shrilled. 'LOOK what you've done to my bicycle! You have made me late for my appointment . . . and Mrs. O'Hara is expecting twins.'

The butcher stared at her in stupification. 'But . . . but you rode straight in front of me!' he managed at last.

Miss Speede drew herself up to her full five foot. 'Young man! I would have you know that I have been travelling these roads for thirty years. I ALWAYS make my crossing at this point . . .'

We heard no more. Aunt Emm and I got busy. With Nutmouse's help, we shepherded the unicorns down the ramp and into the nearest field. It would be a long trail back across open country; we dared not linger. Glancing back, I saw Miss Speede belabouring the cowering butcher with a bicycle pump!

Tripitaka played no part in the rescue. He seemed too interested in Mr. Potts's waving legs. We had not gone far, however, when I heard him coming. His purring was accompanied by a strange, shrill note.

When he caught up, he dropped the object he was carrying at my feet. It was the Weaver's flute!

11. Mirror! Mirror!

*In which Jennifer re-encounters a friend;
certain vices make their ugly mark; and the
Enemy makes a capture.*

Dawn was already breaking when we arrived back, hot and exhausted, at Miss Speede's door. She, herself, had returned long before and fresh as a daisy, once more in her normal shape, was polishing her motor-car. It looked rather smug, I thought, with a plume of steam rising in triumph from its radiator. The Major, fussing and fuming at our absence, was attempting to tidy the yard.

'Do leave that BE, Toby,' Miss Speede kept saying. 'It's fine where it is.'

We all viewed the unicorns with dismay. Their adventure had left them as brittle and transparent as glass!

'My, oh my! You can see right through them,' declared Miss Speede. 'It's windscreen wipers they'll be needing.'

'And we've so far to go,' my aunt said wearily. 'It's fortunate there was no roof to that truck, or they would not be with us.'

'Will they recover?' I felt like crying.

My aunt shrugged. 'They need a tonic, and a rest,' she said.

'You must all stay here until they're better.' Miss Speede was positive.

And stay we did. The long July days stretched sunnily around us, as Aunt Emm and I searched the ditches and hedgerows for watercress and betony, wormwood, plantain and nettle—to be chopped with fennel, thyme and camomile from the old walled garden, and simmered in crab-apple jelly

93

in Miss Speede's large untidy kitchen.

'An old recipe,' my aunt explained. 'Very potent. The "Nine-herbs Charm". It stands against Pain; it dashes against Venom. It is strong against the "Three and Thirty" Evils, against the hand of an Enemy, and against the bewitching of all creatures. The only thing it is powerless to fight is Vanity. And with the unicorns in the state they are there is little likelihood of their suffering from that. Give some to your guinea-pig. It will help to heal his leg.'

She was right; in no time, Squiff was back to his scampering, squeaking self, in a new pen, in the corner of the orchard where we kept the unicorns.

July passed into August. Under the apple-trees, the unicorns grew less brittle. Their coats took on a brighter sheen as they stood lazily flicking their tails beneath the clusters of swelling, moon-washed fruit.

'Apple-trees and moonlight! Just what they need. It's a home from home for them,' Aunt Emm declared happily.

Trip stalked the field-mice in the long grass at their feet; during the day he could be found sunning himself on the top of a delapidated double-decker bus. Nutmouse learnt the skills of a motor mechanic. Clad in a pair of Miss Speede's greasy overalls (far too big for him), he would whistle merrily as he applied spanner to nut, or stuck a patch on a punctured tyre.

The Major, alone, was restless. There were frequent skirmishes when he tried to 'organise' the yard.

Inevitably, the time for parting came. Aunt Emm announced it with regret. 'We must be going soon. We can't stay here for ever.'

I nodded in agreement. After so much activity at the start of our journey, I was beginning to feel bored by the current inactivity.

'It's a lovely day,' I remarked. 'Could I walk into town

to see what's happening? Just for something to do.'

'You can buy some provisions while you're there. We'll start to restock the caravan in preparation for the journey.'

I set off happily, swinging the basket. It was good to be walking again, even only the two miles into town. The air throbbed with the sound of insects. Bees were bumbling heavily amongst the tangle of vetches, buttercups and trefoil by the side of the way. I plucked a dandelion-clock and blew its tiny parachutes into the air—'One-o'clock...two-o'clock...three-o'clock...four!' The seeds floated into the blue sky, on their journey to new beginnings. In somebody's garden? A farmyard? A field? 'Everywhere!' I crowed, shaking the last few seeds from the bald head. I was powerful!

With one breath I could make brand-new yellow flowers, round and bright as medals, green leaves edged with dragon's teeth. There was no room in my beautiful world, I thought, for Mr. Potts and his like. 'Anyway,' I told myself, 'they're gone. They haven't been seen since Miss Speede caused them to crash. We've beaten them. Hurray!'

I spun like a top down the centre of the road, the breeze whistling between the canes of my basket. 'Will you watch where you're going,' shouted a man on a bicycle, wobbling towards the ditch.

I arrived at the town, where people were behaving more sensibly, and settled down to the serious business of shopping. I had been wrong, I thought, to imagine I could find excitement here. It was just the usual small country town, with a row of shops on either side of the main street, an hotel standing up larger than the buildings surrounding it, pubs on every corner, a church in the centre, a small market-square with a memorial to a local hero but without stalls, for it was not market-day. Nothing special. Except, somewhere, somebody was singing, very sweetly, in a high, clear voice.

Having finished my shopping, I followed the sound. It led me up a narrow alleyway beside the church into a second street, away from the busy traffic. A girl was standing by the church railings, head thrown back, a look of serious concentration on her thin pale face as she sang, with eyes half-closed:

> *Eileen, Eileen,*
> *Wait for me.*
> *Wait, my Eileen*

'Maggie!' I cried.

'Jenny, am I glad to see you!' Maggie stopped singing in mid-note. She looked, anxiously, right and left along the street, and over at the windows of a pub opposite, where dark shapes could be seen moving behind the frosted glass. Picking up the man's cap that was lying at her feet with a few coins in it, she took me by the hand and hurried me back to the security of the alley.

'I've been looking out for you,' she whispered. 'I've something to tell you.'

'What?' I asked.

'D'ye see the pub, over there?' She nodded back, along the alley. 'Sweeney's. Well, I was in there, yesterday, with me gran...she had her Guinness, and I had enough left over from the singing for a packet of crisps. There was three men in there. One of them I'd seen before...a big fat fella with dark glasses. The second fella must have been his brother...as like as two peas...only without the glasses. The other man had a nasty mean face, like a rat in a smart city-suit. He seemed to be the boss. They had their heads together, talking.'

'Mr. Potts!' I breathed, recognising the description. 'And *both* Behan brothers! "Evil" must have joined them.'

'Listen,' said Maggie. She gripped my arm. 'I'll have to go back to the singing soon, or me gran will skelp me; she's waiting for her Guinness. Tell the kind lady... the one who gave us the toffees... those men are after her little horses. I couldn't hear all they said, but they were planning dreadful things.'

'Horses!' I stared at Maggie in disbelief. 'But it was broad daylight when you were at the caravan. Only the big mare was showing. How...?' I withdrew my arm.

Maggie bobbed her pigtailed head, twisting the big, rough cap in her hands.

'I see things others can't,' she whispered. 'I don't know how... I always have. My great-gran was the same, Ma says. I don't let on about it, any more... the boys would tease me. Oh, Jenny!' She looked up at me, two fat tears brimming in her big grey eyes. 'They were so beautiful, with their golden horns. I've never seen the like before. Please don't let those wicked men hurt them.'

'No,' I said. 'Of course I won't.' I dug into my purse.

She drew back. 'I don't want it.'

But I insisted. 'All singers get paid, or ought too. Why shouldn't you? You have a lovely voice.'

I turned away. There was a nasty, tight knot in my throat, swelling till it filled my chest. I scarcely heard Maggie's 'Goodbye, Jenny.' Very soft, and sad.

'Are you unwell?' my aunt demanded, over supper. 'You've hardly eaten a thing. Why do you keep opening and shutting your mouth, like a fish?'

'It... it's nothing,' I replied. 'I'm rather tired, that's all. I think I'll go to bed early.'

'Why didn't you tell her? Why didn't you deliver Maggie's message?' demanded a small voice at the back of my head, as I climbed the stairs. There were a great many stairs, as my bedroom was right at the top of the house, in the attic. After the first couple of flights, the piece of narrow red carpet held down by tarnished brass stair-rods, ceased; my feet seemed to stomp out the words on the wooden treads—'Tell her; tell her; tell her.'

'You couldn't,' a second voice assured me (it seemed to come from the space between my eyebrows and to belong more directly to me). 'You couldn't get a word in edgeways, with the Major reminiscing about his campaigns in the Desert?'

This was partly true. Since his enforced 'leave', the Major had been talking a great deal (in order to impress his importance as a 'man of action' upon the ladies, I suspected). His experiences in the Middle East seemed to have little to do with fighting and much to do with flying-carpets, genies in bottles and strange spirits called 'djinns' or 'afreets'. With the aid of whiskey and soda before the meal and brandy after, the Major had been particularly talkative that evening. But, not all the time; there had been gaps in the conversation . . .

'So it's simply not true. Your excuse is feeble,' sneered the first voice.

'Oh shut up!' said the second as I paused at the top of the stairs. 'I'm not going all the way down to tell them, now. It can wait till morning.'

The first voice said nothing. I knew what it was thinking, in its niche at the back of my mind. 'You're jealous! Jealous, because Maggie, the travelling-girl, can see things when you can't.'

'I really *am* tired,' I said, aloud. 'And I *will* tell Aunt Emm tomorrow.'

Tired I might have been. But I could not sleep. After our arrival at Miss Speede's, I had found it hard to readjust to sleeping at night and being active in the daytime. Now, having re-established a more normal routine here I was

choosing to go to bed while it was still daylight. Late
sunbeams played on the other side of the drawn curtains,
beckoning me with golden fingers. Down in the orchard, a
male blackbird was singing (much too loudly). His song was
being repeated by another blackbird, further away; always
three notes behind, like an echo.

I tried to read a book of poems my aunt had lent me, about
cats. They all had names as long as Tripitaka (they had his
perverse habits, too!). The poems were enjoyable, but 'Voice
Number One' kept interrupting with, 'You should have told;
you should have told,' in counter-metre.

I must have fallen asleep while I was still reading, for I
awoke to find myself sitting bolt upright with the pillow and
the book on the floor. I twisted my head around to ease the
crick in my neck. Moonbeams had replaced the sunbeams;
a hunting owl, the blackbird. I listened. There were strange
sounds coming from the orchard.

'Something's the matter,' I thought. I got out of bed and
peeped through the curtains. I could see nothing but the tops
of the apple-trees, undulating like a silvery sea. I put on my
slippers and dressing-gown and slipped downstairs, letting
myself out by the back door.

The unicorns were all gathered at the far end of the
orchard. The moonlight was falling through the trees, forming
weird, jerking patterns on their coats and causing their
shadows to leap and shudder across the grass. They were very
restless; jostling one another, stamping, and squealing in a
manner I had never heard before.

'What is it?' I was frightened. But, at the same time, I
knew that I must try to calm them. I ducked beneath the
fence that divided the orchard and the adjacent field, putting
a strong post and rails between me and the stamping hooves.

'Steady, boy! What's making you so excited?' I spoke
soothingly, offering my hand, palm-upward, to the stallion—
The next moment I had jumped back in alarm for, instead

of nuzzling my hand for a tid-bit as was normal, he flattened his ears and showed his teeth, snatching his head away as if I had threatened him with a whip.

'What is it?' I repeated, in distress. He neighed shrilly, tossing and shaking his head, slicing the shadows with his long horn. Suddenly he wheeled about and, tail held high, smashing between the trees, circled the orchard at a gallop.

'Whoah!' I cried desperately. 'Whoah!' His actions were making the mares frantic. They were pressing against the fence; at any minute, I thought, they would burst through. He came to a halt then, staring, eyes wild, over the rails at something in the field. Until that moment, I had been too occupied by the unicorns to look further. I turned and followed his gaze.

The field had sprouted strange shapes in the night. Round structures, draped in tarpaulin, that looked like giant drums; a tall tower, striped like a massive stick of 'Peg's Leg' peppermint-rock; boats hung on frames; square tents sporting fluttering flags from their bright canvas tops; and words on bunting which, at that distance, I was unable to read.

'Why, it's a fun-fair!' I almost laughed with relief. 'All the fun of the fair. Nothing to be scared of.'

I stopped. The unicorns, I realised, were *not* scared. They were in a state of high excitement, staring avidly at something in the fairground.

A row of mirrors caught my eye; the kind with twisted glass that distort your features when you look in them. They had been left uncovered, leaning against one of the roundabouts. 'How odd!' I thought, 'and how careless.' What was the point of leaving such mirrors around for everyone to have a free look?

'Well, it won't do your vanity much good if you go in there,' I chuckled to the stallion. 'You won't like what you see.'

Vanity! It was all clear in an instant. Vanity was the one thing Aunt Emm's charm had no power to correct. Hastily, I counted the mirrors. There were seven of them; one each, for our depleted herd. Someone had left them for a trap!

I peered at the top of the roundabout where part of the tarpaulin had slipped, exposing a few letters of the owner's name:

—HAN BROS

'—han Bros.' Not much to go on. But enough!

'Shoo! Shoo!' I yelled at the unicorns, dancing in front of them and waving my arms, 'Shoo! Be off!' Alarmed, they scattered, dashing away, bucking and shying, between the trees.

Something was needed to break the mirrors. Such an action would lead to seven years' bad luck, my aunt would probably say. However, it must be done.

There was a pile of metal near the fence; spare parts left over from Miss Speede and Nutmouse's overhauling of a post-van. Near the top was a steel bar, bent at one end for removing hub-caps. I snatched it up, running towards the mirrors as fast as I could before the unicorns should return.

My own reflection reared up in front of me. Hideous! Ears flapping like bat's wings, nose squashed to a pancake, teeth like tombstones. I did not take a second look. I lifted the bar and brought it down, crashing upon the glass.

Splinters flew everywhere, fragmenting the moonlight as they fell. I felt a sharp pain on my wrist, but ignored it, continuing my onslaught upon the mirrors, one by one.

I reached the last. I had only time to hit it once, causing a crooked star to shoot over the surface, before a heavy hand gripped my shoulder, making me drop the bar.

12. In Enemy Hands

In which Jennifer finds herself in serious
trouble; the Major mounts a campaign; and the
Enemy goes around in circles.

'Let me go! Let me go!' I wriggled frantically, but it was useless; the pressure of the hand only grew stronger. It was a large hand, fat and pink as a ham. I twisted round so that I could see the face belonging to it.

They were both there; the Behan brothers—Evil and Chop. Chop had removed his dark glasses. I could see why he found it necessary to wear them, for he had a hideous squint, his eyeballs rolling uncontrollably towards his pug-nose. It was he who held me; his brother did the talking.

'Well well, darlin' girl!' he wheezed pleasantly. 'Meddlin' as usual, I see. Only this time you have been destructive with it. Tut, tut! What will Auntie say when she sees all that broken glass upon the ground? So uncomfortable for tender feet.'

'My aunt would say I had done the right thing,' I replied defiantly.

'Would she now? I know somebody who is not going to be so pleased when he hears his property has been damaged. Bring her along, Chop, that's me boyo.' Together they dragged me, struggling and protesting, towards a long silver caravan parked near the centre of the fairground. Evil Behan knocked.

'Enter,' called a sharp voice.

Mr. Potts was seated at a table in the middle of the van. He did not look up when we entered, being occupied with

seven small bottles and a syringe. He was sterilizing the
syringe over a purple flame. The flame lit his pasty-white
forehead, making it look ice-blue. A lick of hair flopped over
it; blue-black as a raven's wing.

'Have you caught them?' he asked absently.

'Not yet.' The newsvendor shifted uneasily. 'There's been
a slight "hiccup". We have a visitor.' He pushed me forward.

Mr. Potts's pale eyes travelled up till they came to rest
upon my face. His expression changed from one of concentration to intense loathing.

'What's *she* doing here?' he demanded.

Neither brother replied. They stepped back as if trying to
detach themselves from me, and stood swaying ponderously,
like over-inflated punch-balls.

'I've broken your mirrors,' I said, taking matters into my
own hands. 'And I'm glad I did, for you were going to use
them as a trap. How did you know Aunt Emm couldn't
protect the unicorns against vanity?'

'How did I know? You underestimate my powers, my dear.
Not that it takes Great Magic to calculate a unicorn's
weaknesses. Silly frivolous creatures. Fit only for children's
stories! They are of no use until they are dead.'

'What makes you think everything must have a *use*?' I
parried, standing up as straight as I could and staring him
in the eyes. I was aware that I did not present a very dramatic
figure in my dressing-gown and bedroom slippers, but at least
I could say something that would make Aunt Emm proud.

Mr. Potts's thin toothbrush moustache twitched angrily.
He snarled, showing a set of perfect, even teeth. ('Obviously
false,' I thought, 'like the colour of his hair.') Under normal
light, the teeth would have been spotlessly white, like in a
television commercial; the flame of the little burner turned
them blue.

'You are a rude little girl who doesn't understand the *real*
world,' he snapped.

'The *real* world!' Now, I was angry. I forgot about my dressing-gown, too short because I had grown so much that summer; my bedroom slippers, soggy from walking through the orchard grass; I forgot about the big fat men breathing heavily behind me. 'The *real* world is not what people like you would make it,' I told him furiously. 'The real world is full of variety and interest and has a purpose of its own. It's not here for you to use and use, until you've destroyed everything and there is nothing left.'

Mr. Potts's face turned a very unpleasant colour indeed (wishy-washy aquamarine from the paint-box, with dirty water added). His fingers tightened on the syringe.

'Oh, my goodness!' I thought. 'He's going to plunge it into me; inject me with whatever drug—lethal or paralysing—he was preparing for the unicorns.'

Instead he put the needle aside and spoke quite calmly. 'Your hand is bleeding,' he observed. 'Allow me to put some powder on it to stem the flow.'

'No, thank you.' I glanced at my wrist. With all that had happened since, I had forgotten about the cut I had received while smashing the mirrors. Well able to imagine what one of Mr. Potts's powders might do to an open wound, I fumbled in my pocket for a handkerchief to bind it up.

'Why don't you suck it, me darlin'?' Evil Behan suggested helpfully. ''Tis the best way to cure a little scratch.'

'Most likely doesn't care for the taste of blood,' his brother sneered. Standing, grim and silent, in his butcher's blue-and-white striped apron, it was the first time he had spoken since my capture. He was wearing, I noticed with a shudder, a large cleaver in his belt. He sounded impatient. 'We must get on. What do you want us to do with her?' he demanded.

'Do? Lock her up, of course. We'll keep her. There's more than one way of baiting a trap. We'll see what her dear aunt will do when faced with a choice. Her niece? Or the unicorns?'

'She'll choose the unicorns, surely,' commented Evil, 'as set against a slipeen of a girl . . . beggin' your pardon, me dear. But you must agree, I'm sure.'

'That may be the case,' Mr. Potts remarked drily. 'But she won't get the unicorns to move without the child. Jennifer was not taken on the journey for sentimental reasons. She had her function. The silly beasts will only follow a young girl.'

He rose to his feet, and tidied the little bottles into a medicine cupboard hanging on the wall. 'Take her away,' he said dismissively.

They locked me into the back of a small van, using a chain and padlock for extra security (I could hear the chain rattling as they set it in place). It was very dark and cold inside, and smelt foul, having been used at one time by the butcher to transport carcasses. I sat on the bare damp floor, listening to the banging and shouting outside.

'They must be dismantling the fair,' I thought. 'Now that they've taken me prisoner, I suppose they won't risk being found so close to Miss Speede's house. They'll travel further away before they try to negotiate. Oh, what a fool I've been! Why didn't I warn Aunt Emm yesterday, when I had the chance? All I can say is that I've saved the unicorns from immediate danger. But, for how long?'

Presently, the van began to vibrate as someone started the engine; it moved forward slowly and gathered speed as it turned into the road. I began to experience extreme discomfort. The swaying motion combined with the stench in the van churned my stomach. I felt sick.

'I *must* have air,' I thought. I battered on the back of the cab, trying to attract the driver's attention; he merely revved the engine and drove faster. In desperation, I crawled across the jerking tilting floor to examine the door. My groping fingers found the outline of a boarded-up window. The top right-hand corner of the board was rotten; it might be possible to work it loose. With difficulty I stood up and, supporting my body against the inside of the door, began to pick at the rotten wood with my finger-nails.

More than once, the jolting of the van knocked me over; I became bruised black and blue. My finger-tips started to bleed, but I persisted until I had made a hole about the size of a golf-ball, through which burst a channel of fresh air. Collapsing in a heap, I drew great breaths of it. At last, worn out, I fell into an uneasy sleep.

I awoke from a dream in which the unicorns galloped, hornless, between flashing mirrors, chased by the butcher with his cleaver. The van had come to a standstill. Daylight was washing over me, for the doors had been flung open. Through them, I caught a glimpse of a piece of wasteland on the outskirts of a town; the type of place where people dump their old cars and worn-out fridges. Despite the unpleasantness of the site, a group of dour-looking men (hired by Mr. Potts for the purpose, I supposed) were re-erecting the fair. Evil Behan was standing in the doorway, holding an enamel mug and a bowl of something.

'Here's your nice breakfast, me darlin',' he smirked. 'Eat it all up, now, so you'll grow big and strong.'

Feeling famished, I took the bowl eagerly. It contained porridge, on which had been poured a liberal supply of cream sprinkled with brown sugar. I was about to eat, when I recalled the unicorns and the moon-daisies. I set it aside.

'Where are we?' I demanded.

'Never you mind.'

'You won't get Aunt Emm to give up the unicorns,' I said. 'You might as well let me go.'

'You'll stay for as long as the Boss wishes.'

This was getting me nowhere. I looked, longingly, at the porridge, but dared not risk it. 'What's the point of going on with this ridiculous pretence of running a fun-fair, now that I've spoilt your plan by breaking your mirrors?' I asked sourly, gesturing to the scene behind him.

Evil shrugged. Well, there was a slight twitching of fat shoulders, which was probably as near as he could get to a shrug.

'One disguise is as good as another,' he offered. 'It's always as well to have a "cover". Besides,' he sniggered, 'what better method to hide a few unicorns, once we get hold of them, then to turn them into hobby-horses twirling round the carousel. Make a bob or two, before we exterminate them ... Eat your porridge. It's gettin' cold.'

'I don't want it. I'm not hungry.'

'Suit yourself,' wheezed the newsvendor. 'Drink your tea, then.' He slammed the door.

I sat, staring gloomily at the mug in my hand. A small round spotlight beamed in upon it from the hole I had made in the right-hand corner of the door. It showed the milk curdling strangely round the rim of the mug. Suspicious! I set it beside the bowl, and took to watching the tiny dust-specks dancing in the beam of light.

All of a sudden the beam went out, as if someone had drawn the shutters. 'So, here you are!' chirped a voice.

That may not be exactly what he said, but it sounded very like it. 'I'd recognise that chirrup, anywhere,' I thought. It was the Weaver's starling! 'Where have you been?' I demanded. 'We haven't seen you since Lough Sheelin.'

The starling withdrew his head from the hole. Opening his yellow bill, he treated me to his impression of the robin's call. 'Oh, never mind,' I said. 'Can you take a message?'

The bird cocked his head, ruffling his neck-feathers; I could see the sunlight glinting on his mischievous round eye. There was no paper or pencil in the van, so I tore a button off my dressing-gown and held it out to him. 'Take this to Aunt Emm,' I commanded. 'Then, lead her back to me.'

Standing on tip-toe, with my eye pressed to the hole, I watched him fly away with my button in his beak. 'I expect he'll drop it, or take it to his nest,' I thought. There was no reason to suppose the bird could help me. Except—the Weaver had said he was a messenger.

With nothing else to do in that cold dark van, I lay down on the floor. Making myself as comfortable as I could with my head pillowed on my arm, I fell asleep.

When I awoke again, the fair was in full swing. There was laughter and shouting; the creak of machinery; music blared.

'I wish somebody would let me out,' I thought. It was no good knocking. Who would hear me in all that racket? Music, which normally I would have enjoyed, mocked me from outside. The 'top of the pops' played loudly—But not so loudly as to drown a new sound.

I scrambled to my feet. Police sirens were screaming

metallically above the strains of the most recent 'Number One'. 'I'm rescued!' I was jubilant. 'Aunt Emm has sent the police!'

The music ceased; the roundabouts grumbled and fell silent. A loud voice boomed through a speaker:

ATTENTION! THIS IS THE GÁRDAÍ SPEAKING. THERE HAS BEEN A BOMB WARNING. WILL EVERYBODY PLEASE LEAVE THE FAIRGROUND AS QUICKLY AND CALMLY AS POSSIBLE...REPEAT...BOMB ALERT. THERE MAY BE AN EXPLOSIVE DEVICE UPON THE ROUNDABOUT. WILL EVERYONE PLEASE EVACUATE THE SITE.

On hearing this, I flung back my head and laughed aloud. Dancing around my prison, I waved my arms triumphantly in the chilly darkness. He had made some attempt (a very poor one) to disguise his voice, but there was no mistaking it for the Major's!

After that, things happened quickly. The door-chain rattled and thumped, as someone worked on the padlock. A few heaves, and the door burst open to reveal Nutmouse, clad in military uniform with 'Bomb Disposal Unit' printed on the badge upon his cap. Barely taking time to grunt a greeting, he slung screwdriver and wrench back into his bag, turned smartly on his heel, and marched towards the big roundabout. I fell out of the van into the arms of my aunt, disguised as a Ban-Gárda in dark navy and white who, it seemed, had made every attempt to tame her hair beneath trim peaked uniform hat and hairnet; she had failed. As she gave me a hug, wild wisps came loose, dancing merrily round her beaming face.

The Major (a Gárda sergeant) was marching to and fro, issuing orders. 'Arrest those men,' he was shouting. There seemed no shortage of willing hands amongst those who had recently erected the fairground (later, I heard they had been dissatisfied with their wages). Mr. Potts and his two fat

henchmen were grabbed as they were trying to sneak away and brought back. Hand-cuffed, they were conducted to the roundabout and forced to mount horses. Nutmouse, having completed a job upon the engine, leapt out of the way. He looked well satisfied as he put away his tools.

The roundabout began to turn. My last memory of the fair was of the painted animals whirling faster and faster until they were changed into ribbons of red and blue and gold. The faces of the rogues flashed intermittently, looking like three white buttons, before disappearing into the next spin. The music for their ride was not a modern pop-song but an old waltz chosen, I suspected, by my aunt:

> *Round and round*
> *For ever and ever.*
> *We're riding on*
> *Love's Roundabout*

'Was there really a bomb?' I asked, as we climbed into the

shiny patrol-car, driven by a smartly uniformed Miss Speede.

'Of course not,' said my aunt. 'The Company of the Hare have nothing like *that* in their armoury. Bombs are for psychopaths and cowards.'

'Major.' She turned to him. 'You planned an excellent campaign.'

'Thought it was rather good myself,' the Major admitted, blushing modestly as he removed his Gárda cap and laid it on his knee. 'But it was not so fine as the campaign I fought in India. I remember, it was on the North-west Frontier ... there was a certain snake-charmer ...

'Dear Major,' murmured my aunt. 'You'll be glad to hear there will be no more time for stories. We start upon the road again, tomorrow.'

As Miss Speede drew the patrol-car out into the traffic, we were overtaken by Nutmouse, driving an army jeep. The windows of the jeep were open, and the tune he was whistling drifted back to us on the wind:

> *Round and round*
> *For ever and ever.*
> *We're riding on*
> *Love's Roundabout.*

13. The Pedlar

*In which the travellers resume their
journey; and an old friend goes out of his way
to give them a warning.*

Next night, after I had enjoyed a hot bath and a good rest
and we had all celebrated the success of the Major's campaign
with a sumptuous supper, we took leave of our kind hostess.

'I'd like to be coming with you,' she told us regretfully.
'But I can't leave the garage. These pieces of old metal need
me.'

After their long stay in the orchard the unicorns seemed
glad to be on the road. Heads tossing, eyes and horns
sparkling, they raced each other at ever-increasing speed,
making it hard for me to stay ahead of them. 'Keep your
hoofs on the road, there,' called my aunt from the car as a
mare took off, floating like a ball of thistledown over the
hedge to land in a cornfield. Eventually, they settled down
to what the Major described as 'a sensible cavalry-trot'.

We chose our route carefully, to avoid the town where the
fair had been held.

'How long will Mr. Potts and his friends go on spinning?'
I asked Aunt Emm.

'That depends,' she replied. 'Partly on the type of axle-
grease Nutmouse applied to the engine, and partly on what
sort of fair it was in the first place. If, as I suspect, it was
conjured by magic, it will just disappear when its time is
done. In either case, the three gentlemen will come down to
earth with a bump. Let us hope it is hard enough to shake
some sense into them.'

Days of ripening harvest passed as we wended our way north. The cornfields turned from apple-green to gold. It became imperative to make detours in order to dodge the combine-harvesters working late at night.

'Such a noise! Such a grabbing of everything the land can give,' deplored Aunt Emm, covering her ears. 'I can remember corn standing in stooks like silent tents for the mice to invade in the moonlight, big-footed horses working all day with a will to bring the harvest home, stack-yards where the children played, scarlet poppies growing in the wheat, spreading their seeds to be ploughed in for another year, plenty of pickings dropped for the birds, and still enough for everyone.'

'Those were the days,' agreed the Major. 'Machinery has brought only greed and haste.'

The landscape began to change. The broad pastures and wide fields of grain gave place to smaller enclosures, growing potatoes or cabbages, hemmed round by dry-stone walls. Grazing was sparse. The ground had begun to show its bones in the shape of seams of rock above the soil. In the damp hollows, soft rush and mosses reigned supreme.

With a change in the scenery, there came a change in the weather. Rain poured down as if someone had turned on taps in the sky. Through its gush and patter one could hear the creaking and gasping of Aunt Emm's widescreen-wipers, working overtime. Behind the car, the caravan was lost beneath a deluge. We grew used to being permanently soaked. Even when we camped we felt wet, for steam rose in clouds from clothes hanging near the stove and fat water-drops plopped into buckets from several places in the leaking roof. Trip dug himself a nest underneath my bed; any suggestions that he might need to go out were met with spits and growls. The unicorns were wretched; manes plastered to their necks, tails to their haunches, they huddled together and refused to eat.

'I wish I hadn't lost my umbrella,' grieved the Major. Even Nutmouse's offer of souwester hats all round did little to cheer him. 'There is mould growing on the inside of my tent,' he complained.

'I think somebody is following us,' I said. Through the ceaseless patter of the rain, I had been convinced for days that I could hear footsteps, accompanied by the tap-tapping of a stick. Nutmouse seemed to agree with me; he nodded wisely.

'Surely those rogues can't be after us, already,' groaned my aunt.

We moved forward uneasily, ears strained for any unusual sound. The weather did not improve. We splashed through a featureless, wet, grey world, in which nothing showed but the first few feet of puddle-strewn road and the lower stones of the boundary wall, black and dripping in the car headlights. The few trees were stunted and set well apart, offering no shelter. 'Will it ever stop raining?' I thought. 'I wish I hadn't come.'

But it did stop. I awoke one afternoon to unaccustomed brightness, and a silence so intense one felt one could wrap it round one like a blanket. Sunlight was streaming through the caravan windows, running in golden ripples across the ceiling to strike stars in all the chrome fittings. The door was open. Through it wafted intoxicating whiffs of heather-honey and the nutmeg smell of gorse, sprinkled with a faint salty tang from the distant sea. Outside, I could hear my aunt singing as she hung up the washing. 'Let's forget your schedule, Toby,' I heard her call. 'We'll stay here for a day or two, and enjoy ourselves.' Leaping out of bed, I flung on my clothes.

We were parked on a wide moor. As far as the eye could see, the heather-clad bog undulated like a purple sea beneath a cloudless sky. Everything was washed clean and sparkling. Raindrops hung like polished crystals upon the gorse. Dotted amongst the heather, the woolly forms of the sheep looked newly laundered. The road we had come along appeared to have been swept by a broom—and it was quite empty. 'So much for my imagining I could hear somebody following,' I thought.

Tripitaka seemed to have been infected with a type of late-summer madness. He darted around the gorse-bushes, batting at the bees and butterflies with his chocolate paws. He burst through the heather stalks, splitting apart newly spun spiders' webs and upsetting their creators. He made pretence of stalking the unicorns (contentedly grazing at last, my aunt informed me, looking more finely polished than their surroundings). A warning stamp from the stallion sent him packing. Thwarted, he sprang upon Aunt Emm's wash-line and clung, swinging, from one of the Major's shirts.

'For goodness sake, remove that animal before he is court-martialled,' cried my aunt. 'Take him for a long walk.'

It was not so much a case of my taking Trip as of Trip taking me! As soon as we started he shot into the lead, sanity apparently restored, and with the appearance of knowing exactly where he was going. Every hair of his coat bristling with the satisfaction of a cat who has managed to get his own way, he conducted me along a sheep-path, down into a hidden hollow, where grey sallow grew in thickets beside a rushing stream. Above the calmer pools, damsel-flies hung, darting occasionally sideways, like clockwork helicopters. Our arrival disturbed a big grey heron, who flapped away clumsily on wings too broad to manage. Standing, silently contemplating the water on the far side of the stream, was an old man, as lank and grey as the departing bird, his face hidden by the hood of his shabby duffle-coat. I took him to be a tramp, or perhaps a wandering pedlar for he carried a sack upon his back. A narrow white cane, tapping the edge of the bank, proclaimed that that he was blind.

'Don't try to cross,' I called to him. 'I can see some

stepping-stones, downstream. I'll help you.'

'Thank you,' he replied. There was something familiar about his voice but, with my mind engaged in helping him safely across the stones, I let the impression pass.

Once again Trip took charge, this time heading back to camp. 'He hasn't had his meal. He's hungry, I expect,' I told the man.

He nodded, saying nothing as he walked behind me along the narrow path. I could hear the soft thumping of his probing cane. Now and again he halted and whistled like a bird, and buntings and whinchats came flocking through the heather at his call. We arrived at camp in a cloud of chirping birds.

The effect of our appearance upon the others staggered me. The unicorns all whinnied. Nutmouse sprang to his feet, doffing his cap-of-the-moment and making a low bow. The Major stood stiffly to attention and saluted. Squiff (in his pen) almost burst his sides with his shrill guinea-pig 'whistles'. 'Oh!' exclaimed my aunt. 'You've come! You are most welcome.' She advanced towards the visitor, hand outstretched.

As he took my aunt's hand, the pedlar's hood fell back to reveal fine features, blue eyes, and long white hair.

'I . . . I'm very sorry. I didn't recognise you,' I stammered.

'Why should you?' smiled the Weaver. 'It is some time since we met. You have been doing well, I hear. A certain starling has been keeping me informed. His language is florid, but one can pick out the truth, like corns of barley, from amongst the chaff of his chatter.'

'I haven't done well at all,' I burst out. 'I've made some dreadful mistakes.'

'Mistakes!' The Weaver brushed them lightly aside. 'A mistake is just an everyday pitfall. Something you climb out of, before you go on trying. You must not wallow in your mistakes.'

'Come and sit down,' my aunt urged him. 'You must be tired after your long journey. I will prepare an early supper.'

Long after the meal was finished, we sat watching the sun dropping towards the west and the stars appearing; first one and then another, pinpricks in the still luminous sky. The moon arose, thin and bent as the paring of a finger-nail.

'A new month is beginning,' whispered my aunt. 'We must make a wish.'

I glanced towards the gorse clump where Trip had been making mischief earlier. The unicorns, as yet as faint to me as soap-bubbles, were standing very still; eyes wide, horns raised in silent homage to the crescent moon.

The Major was spoiling the magic of the evening by repeatedly clearing his throat. 'Not yet. No questions yet, Toby,' my aunt kept warning him.

'You are wondering why I came.' The Weaver broke his silence. He reached out to take another sip of Aunt Emm's elderflower champagne (kept only for special occasions), then returned to stroking Trip, curled like a chocolate-cream puff upon his knee.

'I did not start in your direction,' he told us. 'I was on my way to pay a visit to the Seal-woman of the West, when I heard news that disturbed me and caused me to take your road. I had stopped off at Tara when Owl came to me with a message. He had seen "Eughan Potts" (we will call him that, for so he is known at present) at darkest midnight on the slopes of Slieve-na-Calliagh. He was searching for a root I will not name, and vowing vengence.

'Wise-woman!' He turned to my aunt. 'If you have a fault, it is this; you are too ready to give the Enemy a second chance. When you had him in your power you should have sent him whirling into space. Now, he is humiliated and angry . . . . I warn you. You will have to pass Finnoe. Beware! Go round it. On no account allow your charges to enter under the trees.'

'Finnoe...'"The Wood of the Yew". Just the place for Eughan Potts,' murmured my aunt. 'Oh yes, I see...I will remember,' she assured the Weaver.

I was growing sleepy, barely hearing what was being said. One thing, however, had been bothering me, and I felt that I must ask.

'Please,' I said timidly, stretching out my hand to touch the Weaver's sleeve. 'When we find the island, how do we get the unicorns across the sea? The newsvendor said they couldn't swim. Will there be a boat?'

'No boat can land on Inishnallis. But, do not worry.' Gently, the Weaver lifted Squiff from where he was nestling on my shoulder, bright eyes peeping at us from behind my hair. He held the little creature in the palm of his hand, examining the fur-clad body with his tender fingers. 'Everyone on this journey has a job to do, even the smallest,' he told us. 'There is a way to cross to Inishnallis. It is kept hidden. But this little animal will be allowed to find it.'

'Where exactly *is* Inishnallis?' the Major enquired. 'It isn't marked on any of my maps.'

The Weaver delved into his sack, bringing out a strange blue-green stone like a crystallised splash of sea water. 'Add this to your compass,' he said. 'When you reach the shore, press it to the flying-horse's forehead beneath his mane. The island will be drawn towards you.'

Next morning the Weaver—turned pedlar once again— opened his sack, spreading his wares upon the ground.

'Such lovely things! I wish I had some pocket-money,' I sighed wistfully.

'No money needed.' The old man pressed a gift into my hand. It was a tiny unicorn delicately carved from milk-white stone.

'This is for the Future,' he told me, 'to remind you of the Past. For the Present, you will require something more practical.'

He let his hand run over necklaces with beads like drops of foam; quaint stones carved to look like beetles; small hand-mirrors reflecting the blue sky; coloured ribbons like rainbows. Finally he handed me a little alabaster pot. It contained some amber-coloured ointment, smelling of marigolds, apple-mint, angelica, and other herbs I could not name. 'Use this sparingly, and only when it is really necessary,' he instructed me.

There was a label attached to the lid of the pot. Squinting at the small red print, I read: *Use as instructed. Rub to the right for growth; to the left for shrinkage. KEEP AWAY FROM UNKIND HANDS!*

It was not as pretty a gift as the little unicorn, nor could I see the need for it. But I thanked him politely and put it in my pocket.

14. The Wood of the Yew

*In which the brothers Behan undergo a
transformation; Mr. Potts conducts an experiment;
and Jennifer foils the Enemy.*

The days that followed the Weaver's visit were purple and
pale-blue and gold, the nights ink-blue and silver-spangled,
as we trekked over the burgundy-coloured bog. The wild
countryside suited the unicorns. They were in lively mood,
romping away across the heather. Often I had to perform a
whole repertoire of bird song to bring them back again.

'No sign of the Wood,' said my aunt with relief, as we
camped one morning.

'Nor of the Enemy,' I said. 'Perhaps Owl was mistaken.'

The Major said nothing. He passed me his telescope and
pointed upwards. High overhead, a big black bird (a raven,
perhaps?) floated in the clear sky, watching us.

The next night the moon rose and the stars came out as
usual. But later, storm-clouds gathered to blot them away,
and distant thunder rumbled.

Suddenly we were lashed by a downpour. A sheet of blue-
white lightning floodlit the landscape. It revealed the jagged
outline of some trees not far from where we stood. The
CRASH that came after sent the unicorns hurtling towards the
trees like a herd of frightened deer. I followed close behind.
I have always been scared of thunder and, exposed as we were
on the bare moor, I could do nothing but scamper blindly
and stupidly for cover.

Twigs whipped my face, but I ran on. Now and again, a
flicker of lightning would show trees bending towards me like

121

thin black men. Beyond them, like flitting spectres, galloped the white forms of the unicorns. Panic was at my heels. I dared not stop. I could not return to the open; I could not stand still amongst those trees that creaked and jerked, like an army of skeletons about to grab me. At the back of my whirling mind, something told me I must keep pace with the unicorns.

It was not to be! My foot was caught by a gnarled root and I was sent sprawling. By the time I sat up and regained my breath, the herd had passed. I was alone.

Painfully I stood up. The storm was rolling away, but it was still pitch-dark. How I wished I carried a torch! Then I remembered the Major had entrusted me, earlier, with the Weaver's compass; I had it in my pocket. The thunder-storm must have affected it, for it emitted only a feeble glow that lit nothing. Nevertheless, it gave me courage. With one hand outstretched to ward off whatever might come at me, I proceeded forward.

A strange red light filtering through the trees attracted my attention. Hoping it might be the dawn, seen through the end of the wood, I crept towards it, parting the fir branches.

What I saw held me rivetted to the spot with horror!

The Behan brothers and Mr. Potts were seated on the ground in the centre of a clearing. It might have been supposed they were gathered for a picnic, for Mr. Potts was cooking something on a barbecue—Except for the fact that Evil and Chop were bound tightly, hand and foot! Whatever Mr. Potts was cooking it smelt revolting, like a mixture of bad eggs and rotten parsnips. It did not sizzle on the grill; it screamed as if tormented.

The light from the fire caught a mad look in Mr. Potts's watery pale eyes, as he turned and prodded the shrieking vegetable with his fork. Two livid spots on his sallow cheeks gave the lie to his usual cool exterior, hinting of high excitement underneath.

'Never in all my years as a chemist have I had the chance to attempt this experiment!' he gloated. 'Two overweight, small-brained men are not going to stop me now.'

'I only said I hoped it tasted better than it smelt,' Evil protested. He broke off in a paroxysm of coughing, as fumes from the barbecue were blown in his direction. 'I don't see why we have to be tied up like common criminals,' he managed to grumble.

'This root is rare; I cannot afford to waste any,' Mr. Potts replied crisply. 'The experiment requires absolute compliance on your part, and I don't trust you. Besides, your brother might turn violent again.'

'He always had a bit of a temper,' the newsvendor confirmed fawningly. 'But he'll do as you say, now. Won't you, Chop?'

The butcher snarled. Opening his mouth he began to hurl a string of uncomplimentary words at Mr. Potts. The abuse was cut short in a gurgle. Mr. Potts seized him firmly by his snub nose. Spearing a piece of root with his fork, he rammed it down the gasping butcher's throat.

Choking, the man fought violently. He squirmed, trying to break his bonds. Large though he was, he was powerless. Mr. Potts caught him, deftly, beneath the double chins. Tipping his head back, he forced him to swallow.

'Mercy!' gasped Evil as he saw the chemist advancing. Sweat ran in rivulets down his ashen, flabby cheeks, blackening his collar. Mr. Potts ignored his pleas. He speared a second morsel, treating the newsvendor like his brother. Evil tried to spit it out, but with the same merciless tipping back of the head Mr. Potts make sure that he, too, swallowed.

Aghast, I watched. For an instant, the two men froze, mouths gaping, eyes bulging, like a pair of frogs. The sweat oozing from their foreheads seemed to be melting them. Tied as they were in a crouching position, they appeared to shrink lower. At the same time they spread outwards, so that they

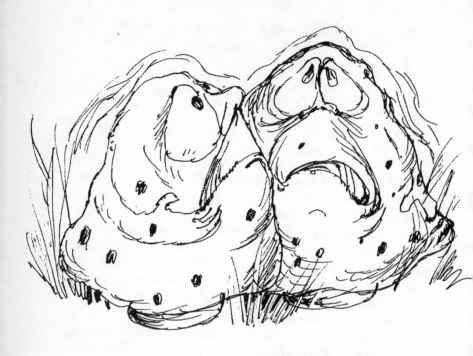

were flabbier than ever. Their faces turned a lurid yellow. Slowly, almost imperceptibly, they were changed into toadstools.

A sound made me turn my attention back to Mr. Potts. Once again he was bent over the barbecue, engrossed in his culinary skills. Some sort of spice was produced from a leather pouch and sprinkled on the remaining root; a piece of honeycomb was added. Finally the chemist stood up, dousing the whole with liquid from a flask. Green flames sprang upwards. Hastily removing his jacket, Mr. Potts rolled up spotless white shirt-sleeves. Plunging his bare arm through the flame, he drew out the last piece of root. He waited for it to cool, examining it, critically, on the end of the fork. He sniffed, testing the aroma. Taking a deep breath, he commenced to chant:

White Bryony; rare plant;
Mandragora's brother.
Root of Man's shape,
Change me to another.
Sap, for my blood flow.
Bough, take for arm.
Feet into roots, grow.
Change me, Green Charm!

Fastidiously, like a gourmet sampling a new dish, he started to nibble the root.

The result was immediate and shocking! Mr. Pott's pale face darkened to a deep shade of green. His black hair floated up and out, changing to foliage. His arms rose up, sprouting feathery fronds. Where his finger-tips had been, there hung scarlet berries. His smartly shirted chest and immaculately trousered legs became welded into one long piece, covering themselves with a coarse coating of reddish-brown bark...

I did not wait for the end of the transformation. Uttering a scream, I fled. Bursting out of the wood I collided with my anxious aunt.

'Aunt Emm! Aunt Emm.' It took me a time to get out the words, 'Mr. Potts is in that wood. Oh, Aunt Emm! He's changing into a tree.'

My aunt remained remarkably calm. 'The Wood of Finoe!' she said. 'There is no need to ask what sort of tree he has become.'

She held me firmly by the shoulders until I could control my trembling. 'Where are the unicorns, Jennifer?' she asked quietly.

'I haven't seen them for some time. They're in the wood,' I said. My voice was small.

'Have you the Weaver's gift? The ointment?'

I nodded. Dumbly I turned back. I knew what I had to do.

The sky had cleared by the time I re-entered the wood.

The moon gave sufficient light to pick a way through the trees. I clutched my alabaster pot tightly in my hand. 'Now, is the time to use it,' my aunt had said.

I had little difficulty finding the glade where I had come across Mr. Potts. Sounds of snorting and tramping there told me that where I had last seen the Enemy, I would find the unicorns.

The place had changed. A large yew-tree now stood in the centre of the clearing. Where its outer branches dipped almost to the ground, there sprouted two plump and particularly poisonous-looking toadstools. I glimpsed them only for a moment between the trampling hooves.

For the whole area was a-surge with movement!

Fear in their eyes, the unicorns were wheeling to and fro across the clearing. They looked, I thought, as if they were being drawn on invisible strings. At first, I was unable to make out the cause of their anxiety. Then the sea of frantic bodies parted, offering me a view.

The stallion was twisting and jerking in the midst of all, his feet pounding the ground in a mad dance as he struggled to release his horn from the hard trunk of the tree.

'MR. POTTS! LET GO. I KNOW IT'S YOU.'

My voice sounded shrill—unnatural. It split the scene. The mares reared, shuddering to a halt. In the silence that followed, I could hear their tortured breathing.

Eventually the stillness was broken by the milk-white mare. Stretching out her neck, she nervously began to sniff at the toadstools.

'Don't touch them! They're *poisonous*!' I cried, agonised.

The mare shied, her hooves stamping the toadstools into pulp. The others took her sudden movement as a signal; snorting, they turned and galloped off into the wood.

I stared in horror at the glutinous yellow mass that had been the Behan brothers. Under the tree the stallion stood very still, his back hunched, his neck dripping sweat.

'Mr. Potts! If you don't let go, you're going to regret it.'
Fighting the terror in my voice, I forced myself to speak
calmly. It was difficult, for beneath the branches of the tree
the air was chill. My teeth were chattering. My fingers felt
numb as I unscrewed the top of the alabaster jar.

'To the left for shrinkage.'

Taking a little of the ointment on my finger-tip, I rubbed
it into the bark close to the spot where the unicorn's horn
was trapped, smoothing it, as instructed, in an anti-clockwise
direction.

The tree shrieked and groaned, lashing with its branches
like a demented fiend. Fat scarlet berries pattered on to our
backs, staining the unicorn's white coat like drops of blood.

'Use sparingly,' the Weaver had said. Did I dare apply
more? There was no need—the red-brown bark of the tree
was splitting open? Foot by foot the stallion stepped back.
His horn slipped from the yew-tree's trunk like a knife from
butter. He was *free*.

But I was caught! The sharp twigs of the tree had grabbed my hair, looping it strand by strand round their wooden fingers, refusing to let go.

'HELP! HELP!' Fires burned in my scalp as I fought to escape. Above me, the dark foliage of the tree hissed and soughed. I swear it laughed.

Suddenly I heard the sound of someone crashing through the undergrowth. Nutmouse loomed into view, his bewhiskered visage grim, his brown hand grasping a woodman's axe. He lifted it high above his head. I saw the sharp blade flash as it whistled downward to bite into the yew-tree's roots.

The tree swayed, releasing its grip. Its cries were terrible. The rasping groan of splintering wood sounded human, horribly human! I crawled from under its tormented branches. Once clear of the icy shadows I looked up and saw that the stallion was waiting for me. He bent his head. I wound my fingers into his long, crisp mane. He stood quite still, allowing me to climb upon his back.

I rode as in a dream. 'Yes,' I might say later, 'I've ridden on a unicorn...but I can't...quite...remember what it felt like....'

When we came out on to the heather, the mares gathered round us. I patted my steed's firm silky neck, and slid from his back. Morning was approaching and a mist was rising from the ground. The herd moved away, melting into its soft damp folds.

'Miaow,' Tripitaka was staring up at me with his squinting eyes.

'Oh, Trip! Dear old Trip!' Picking him up, I buried my face in his warm honey-beige fur. He protested, volubly, when I burst into tears.

15. The Kings of the Sea

*In which, the Enemy dispatched, the
travellers find themselves faced with a final obstacle;
and Squew-wiff sorts out a problem.*

We stood at the edge of the cliff, looking down on the strand
below. The tide was running white between us and the island,
and great grey seals were basking on the strand.

'Kings of the Sea,' my aunt had called them. They did not
look particularly king-like to me, but their dark liquid eyes,
gazing up at us with curiosity, were beautiful.

Three days earlier, Aunt Emm had driven Mr. Potts, his
feet swathed in bandages and equipped with a pair of
crutches, to the nearest railway-station to await the once-a-
day train.

'A few toes missing! He was lucky to get away with THAT,'
she said. 'It will put an end to his wandering for the time
being.'

'Wasn't it awful about the newsvendor and his brother?'
For the first time, I felt able to speak of the matter.

'It was,' said my aunt. 'They were poisonous men, and they
ended as poison. However, even if the unicorns had not
trampled upon them, they were doomed. Mr. Potts had every
intention that they should be eaten, so as to kill the unicorns
to satisfy his greed for their horns. I suppose he would have
taken their hooves too. And any other pieces that might have
been useful to his chemistry.'

I shuddered. 'Perhaps it would have been better if
Nutmouse had gone on chopping with his axe,' I suggested.

'Perhaps,' replied Aunt Emm. 'But he never could have

done it. Like all of us, he finds it hard to be destructive.'

Thanks to the use of the Weaver's stone, we found the Island quite easily. But now, with the sea frothing and churning like milk, we could see no way to reach it.

'Inishnallis—the Island of the White Stream,' mused by aunt. 'It is well-named.'

'We can't stay here, kicking our heels, for ever.' The Major was getting fidgetty.

'I'm hungry,' I complained.

'We'll have a picnic while we decide what to do,' said Aunt Emm.

The grass on the cliff-top was soft and springy, warmed by the sunshine and scented with small flowers. Sheep's sorrel and cinquefoil peppered the ground. After they had eaten, the others fell asleep. I sat with my chin on my hands, gazing at the Island before me, rising, green slopes gleaming like emeralds, out of the chopping waves. Whenever a cloud blew over, it seemed to shift and change colour and shape. It looked as if it could float away at any moment—'As well, it might,' I thought, remembering the legends. Plucking a protesting Squew-wiff away from his grazing, I popped him into my pocket and walked to the cliff-edge.

The seals were swaying to and fro, looking up at me with their dewy eyes and calling. The cries they made were impelling, like a summons. Cautiously I crept nearer to the rim of the precipice and peeped over. There was a path, very narrow and very steep, running down to the beach, just a few feet from where I stood. 'Here goes!' I thought, and lowered myself over the edge.

Fifteen minutes later, hot, dusty, with scuffed shoes and little beads of blood bubbling on one of my elbows, I reached the shore. On my approach the seals, who had been watching me all the time, uttered clamorous cries and made their way clumsily into the water. Once in that element they became truly regal, swimming with a grace and energy that was breath-

taking, through the pounding waves towards a rocky promontory that jutted from the cliff.

'Wait!' I shouted. 'Wait.' I began to run along the shore. The last of their number half-lifted herself from the water, turned her pointed snout towards me and eyed me inquisitively, before sinking out of sight to join her brothers.

I came to the promontory short of breath. A water-wagtail flew up from under my feet and settled again further up the strand, his tail pumping urgently. Nothing else moved. The rock towered above my head like a fortress; impregnable, blind, switched in on itself, hiding its secrets from the midday sun. I turned my back on it and sat on the hot sand, once more concentrating my attention upon the Island. It had changed again, becoming flatter and donning a rainbow like a multi-coloured coat.

'Please don't float away until we have the unicorns safely on you,' I whispered.

I must have fallen asleep, for I was awoken by the sound of voices. I could not understand what they were saying for they spoke in a foreign language, but it became obvious to me, after a time, that there were many people speaking and that their voices came from inside the rock.

This startling discovery dwindled to unimportance when I put my hand in my pocket and discovered that Squiff was no longer there! He had been safely crouched underneath my handkerchief when we reached the bottom of the cliff. I knew, for I had checked. Desperately I looked around. Even the wagtail was gone. There was nothing but bare sand shimmering in the heat and the pounding waves.

The voices chattered on. Behind the rocky wall somebody laughed, and a stringed instrument began to play. 'Someone must be having a party,' I thought sourly. I looked down and noticed some disturbance of the sand at the foot of the rock. It led to a crack just wide enough for a small animal to creep through. Down on my hands and knees I explored the crack with my fingers. Nothing! The voices grew louder and more distinct. Someone began to sing. A boy's voice—clear, unearthly, beautiful. I eased myself on to my stomach and with great difficulty applied my eye to the crack.

Indeed, they were having a party! The cave was bright with candles. Stalagmites met stalactites in convoluting columns, like pillars round a hall. Here and there a lump of rock formed a table or a throne-shaped chair. The tables were brimming to the edges with food and drink; a few elderly ladies and gentlemen sat upon the chairs.

But most of the people in that bright hall were young. They stood in groups, chatting and sharing jokes, and toasted one another with wine sparkling in crystal glasses. In the centre of the silvery floor, couples were dancing. A boy, his fair hair tumbling to his shoulders, was singing to the accompaniment of a harp. Now and again, the festivities would break off as the revellers turned to greet a newcomer. He would splash his way through the froth-fringed door and toss aside his drab grey coat to reveal a changed figure, splendid in brightly coloured fine-wool garments, crowned with a band of gold.

Gradually, the meaning of what I was watching dawned in my mind. I had heard stories of the Selchies—the Seal-people—descendants of the children of a long-ago king of Norway, who had been doomed by their jealous stepmother to live their lives as seals, returning occasionally to human form. These colourful, joyful people, I surmised, were the same seals which had called to me from the shore.

Amongst the many small pages who moved among the guests, fetching and carrying and offering food and wine, one in particular caught my eye. This lad was different from his

fellows. Shorter and stouter, with a strange spiky hairstyle that looked to me as if it had been dyed; one half white, the other chestnut-brown with streaks of black. 'I've seen that colouring before,' I thought. 'Quite recently—on a guinea-pig!'

For all his odd appearance, the boy seemed popular. The older people smiled at him and when, carelessly, he dropped a plate of cakes upon the floor everyone laughed, and a tall blond man clapped him on the back and spoke to him kindly. After that, it seemed, he was excused from duties. A place was found for him on a rocky stool, and a plate of biscuits was pressed into his hands. Presently, a graceful lady in a pale green gown came to him and took him by the hand. She led him to where an old gentleman with a long grey beard was seated on the biggest throne.

The page bowed low. He seemed to be asking for something but the king shook his head, unable to understand. The boy thought for a while. Then he began to act a little mime. Intrigued, I watched as details of our journey were displayed for all to see. I recognised the shoeing of the unicorns; the traveller stealing the mare; the horse fair and Nutmeg with his packet of leaves; the gamekeeper, with gun raised; Miss Speede in her car, travelling fast; the fun-fair and its whirling roundabout; Mr. Potts transforming himself into a tree.

The people in the hall stopped talking and gathered round to watch. They clapped. The old king smiled, and stroked his beard. When the performance came to an end, he took a ring from his finger and offered it to the boy, who bowed his thanks but shook his head. He was pink in the face from his exertions, and his skewbald hair stood out spikier than before. He pointed towards the door and out to sea, forming the shape of the Island, urgently, with his hands. Everyone fell quiet and watched the king; the lady in green said something to him.

He pondered for a moment; then clapped his hands, giving orders. Pages fetched brooms and began to sweep the sand from the centre of the floor. I craned to see the outcome of their efforts. It was impossible. My neck was aching from holding my head so long in one position.

'Hoy! Jennifer, what are you doing?'

The lights went out; the hall was plunged into darkness. With the cries of the seals echoing in my ears, I turned to find the Major looking down at me.

'Just thought I'd take a walk,' he said. 'Good for the brain when sorting out a problem.'

'There's no need.' I was jubilant as I gathered my small skewbald guinea-pig into my hands. 'Squew-wiff has done that for us.'

'What's he got, tied round his neck?' The Major bent to look.

I unfastened the knot of pale green wool, releasing the guinea-pig from his burden.

'It's a key,' I said. 'It was hidden in the cave. The Selchies gave it to him. Unless I'm mistaken it will unlock a door to a passage leading to the Island.'

16. Inishnallis

*In which the journey comes to an end;
Jennifer and Aunt Emm say farewell to Nutmouse
and the Major; and the Island disappears.*

'Well, Jennifer! I realise that you have an exceptional guinea-pig, and it was very kind of him to visit the Selchies and acquire the key to a passage beneath the sea. But I don't see how it can help us, when we cannot get through that hole.'

My aunt was looking flustered. Her hair was frizzing away from her head, like a bird's nest that has been submitted to an electric charge. She made an attempt to pat it smooth and it caught in one of her carbuncle rings. 'Ouch!' she added.

'If that mist comes inland the Island will disappear, and we'll miss our chance,' the Major said anxiously. 'As I told you; timing is crucial.'

It had been a difficult task guiding the unicorns down the cliff-path, and it had taken us longer than we had anticipated. A mist had gathered out to sea. Now the tide was in, and the large seaward-facing mouth of the cave was blocked; there was only the little split in the rock through which Squew-wiff had crawled.

'I still have some of the ointment left,' I said. 'Shall I try?'

My aunt nodded. 'Clockwise,' she said.

I rubbed the ointment on to the right-hand edge of the crack and waited. Nothing happened. I scooped the very last traces from the bottom of the jar, and tried again. With a groan, the crack began to lengthen and grow wide—just wide enough for us to squeeze through, one by one. 'Giddy-up!' The Major gave the stallion a push.

Save for a watery light filtering through from the entrance, the cave was dark. The candles were all gone, the rocky tables and chairs were bare. Small waves sucked at the sand, and licked the feet of the outermost pillars. They had washed away all footprints and smoothed out the marks of the brooms; there was no trace of a trapdoor.

'Here! In the centre. We must dig.'

Nutmouse, as always, produced what we needed from nowhere, and bent with his spade to the task. He was hampered by the unicorns jostling him and pressing around.

'Stand back, the Cavalry!' ordered the Major. 'This is a job for the Sappers.'

At last our anxious ears heard the sound we awaited. The 'clink' of metal on metal, steel against brass. We all fell to our knees, pushing aside the sand with our hands. The smooth rectangular shape of a trapdoor was uncovered. There was a keyhole and a brass ring at one end. Brushing away the last of the sand, I inserted the key and turned it. The Major's strong hand reached out and pulled at the ring. The trapdoor came up, silently and easily as if newly oiled.

'Steady now. Don't rush. Take your time.'

The Major's flash-light illumined the first few treads of some stairs, going down. Mercifully, they looked broad enough for the unicorns to manage. 'Take the compass and flute, Jennifer,' he ordered, 'and lead on.'

A soft breeze was blowing along the passage, carrying the spicy scents of gorse and thyme, the sweet aromas of honeysuckle and wild rose. Presently, the monotonous murmur of the tide above our heads was replaced by the twittering of birds. We stepped out into the sun.

The mist had gone, floating away towards the mainland. The Island was so bright, it dazzled!

'Oh!' said Aunt Emm. It was all she could say at first. Then, 'Just right!'

'By Jove! This is the *place*.' The Major took a deep breath;

his moustache rippled. 'One can BREATHE.'

I said nothing. I just looked and looked.

There was everything that was best of all four seasons. Midwinter snow capped the peak of the single mountain. Somehow I knew it would be crisp and powdery, and just right for snowballs. Somewhere up there, too, would be a glacier fringed with icicles, where perhaps a Yeti roamed? Over a narrow river valley hung the blue mists of autumn, streaked with gold. The leaves on the sweet chestnuts had turned to rust, and there were crimson brambles laden with blackberries. When I borrowed the Major's telescope, I could see red, black, and grey squirrels in a yellow hazel-copse, feeding on nuts. Summer was full-blown, with wild roses clambering everywhere, bumble bees in honeysuckle, and myriads of butterflies. Spring lingered in the shape of pussy-willows, fat and soft as small grey paws, frog-spawn like speckled jelly in the pools, primroses and violets beneath the banks, meadows of wild daffodil.

Everywhere there were eyes. Bright beady eyes of woodmice, scuffling for fungus beneath a rotten log; the mild melting eyes of roe-deer, turning to look at us from the meadow; the yellow-rimmed eyes of blackbirds; the smoky eye of a jackdaw; the china-blue eyes of a jay. Round eyes, slanting eyes; eyes that twinkled, eyes that winked. And voices! Soft coos, sharp barks, grunts and snuffles, calls and songs. And movement! The branches of a larch-wood parted to reveal the broad antlers of a stag; flocks of birds wheeled and fluttered in the sky; hares danced and boxed upon the hillside; rabbits scuttled in the wood. There was a rustling in the grass as an inquisitive hedgehog came over to investigate; when he saw Tripitaka, he became a spiky ball.

'Look!' I cried, as a colourful bird trailing a tail of fire flashed across a clearing. 'Was that a phoenix?'

'I expect so,' said my aunt. 'And, there,' she pointed, triumphantly, 'is the Great Irish Elk!'

The unicorns were impatient to be off, but Nutmouse would not let them go until he had removed their shoes, tossing them one by one over his shoulder into the sea, where they gleamed for a moment like a shoal of silver fish before sinking to the depths.

'I shall build my headquarters here.' Already, the Major was busy making a 'recky'. 'Do you think the Weaver could spare you for a time?' He turned to Nutmouse. 'I shall need some help to get established.'

The next few days passed in a frenzy of activity, as we came and went along the passage carrying everything that the Major and Nutmouse might need on the Island.

'It will take only a change in the wind, a turn of the tide, and they'll be gone,' Aunt Emm told me breathlessly. 'Hurry with that first-aid kit, Jennifer. Hurry!'

When it happened, the disappearance took me completely by surprise. One moment the Island was there. Then the mist rolled in from the sea, briefly and unexpectedly, while Aunt Emm and I were on the shore. When it lifted, the Island had vanished.

'The Major's forgotten his balaclava helmet.' My numbed fingers twisted it between my hands.

'Never mind. He won't be needing it. And if he does, Nutmouse can always produce one from the air.'

My aunt's voice sounded choked and strange. She blew her nose noisily on her silk handkerchief. 'That was a good job well done,' she said at last. 'It's time to go home. Where's that guinea-pig? And that cat?'

The journey back across Ireland was amazingly quick and uneventful. Just Aunt Emm and I in the front of the car, with Tripitaka and Squew-wiff sharing the back seat. My aunt and I did not talk much. We spent one night at Gertrude Speede's, and were happy to sit and listen to her chatter.

'The Major always had a screw loose,' she stated. 'Fancy wanting to live the rest of your life on a floating island!'

'It was beautiful,' I said. 'But there were no motor-cars. You wouldn't like it.'

My aunt's house felt cold and damp and sad. However, once the Aga had been relit (under Trip's anxious supervision), and the flames of a small fire sent their reflections dancing on the china ornaments in her sitting-room, the place felt homely again.

'The nights are drawing in,' commented Aunt Emm. 'Tomorrow we must fetch the bees. We have a lot to tell them.'

'It's September,' I said. 'Soon I'll be going back to school.'

Evil Behan's kiosk was shuttered and barred. There was a large FOR SALE board hanging above Mr. Potts's front gate. Rumour had it that he was going abroad, for the sake of his health.

'What mischief will he get up to, there?' sighed my aunt. 'Still, it is out of my territory. The Weaver will look after it. I must send Nutmouse with a few messages when the Major can spare him.'

Save the Unicorns

We sat in silence for a while, listening to the wind gathering power and blowing down the chimney. Above, on the roof, a loose slate rattled.

'Whoosh!' went the wind. 'Clonk!' flapped the slate. 'Whoosh and Clonk!'

'It sounds like the Weaver's loom,' I remarked.

My aunt laughed. 'Perhaps it is,' she said.

Peace was shattered by the ringing of the telephone-bell—an alien sound in my aunt's house.

'You answer it,' she said. 'I can't abide that thing.'

'Jennifer? Where have you been? I've been trying to ring you for days.' It was my mother. 'Did you have a good time?' she asked. 'I hope you weren't bored with Aunt Emm.'

'No,' I said. 'I wasn't bored.'

'Get packed,' she said. 'Daddy and I are coming for you tomorrow.'

'Mum,' I said, 'I've got a guinea-pig. His name is...' There was a click. She had put down the receiver.

I went upstairs. My suitcase was half-packed, anyway. Gloomily, I pulled out drawers and tipped the contents in. Untidy! Not a bit like me.

However, several small packages in tissue-paper merited more careful treatment. They contained a flute, a compass in the shape of a flying-horse, an empty alabaster pot, still smelling faintly of herbs, and a small stone unicorn.

'Add this to your collection. You have earned it.'

I had not heard my aunt come into the room. I opened the small box she gave me. A little gold hare glowed warmly in a bed of cotton-gauze.

'Oh!' I breathed. 'OH!'

'Put it on,' said my aunt. 'You are one of us now.'

Stammering my thanks, I undid the clasp of the chain and hung the charm around my neck. The next moment, I was reeling; almost into my suitcase. The charm must have given me the power of Sight. For, there they were—

The Major! With a slide-rule and sheaf of papers; giving orders. Nutmouse! Up the ladder; laying the thatch.

I looked beyond the newly built cottage, and its already immaculate garden, and up the flowery slopes of the hill. The unicorns were spread out amongst the wild thyme and the orchids, grazing happily. There was the stallion, his magnificent horn gleaming in that incredible sunlight. There were the mares, white and piebald—one; two; three; four; five; six.

And, one other!

By the side of the milk-white mare, his horn no more than a bead of amber on his forehead, pranced a tiny jet-black foal. His feet were *not* upon the ground!

SHELAGH JONES was born in London of Irish-Scottish parentage. Much of her early life was spent on the move — Sussex, Somerset, Angus, Edinburgh, Kent, Perthshire, Yorkshire, Hertfordshire — before she eventually returned to the land of her paternal ancestors, to County Wicklow, where she now lives with four cats, a long-suffering dog, and an even more long-suffering husband. She has one grown-up daughter.

A trained teacher of drama, she has been involved with amateur theatre for many years, first in Scotland, then in Ireland, and still enjoys directing plays. This interest is now shared with sitting at a typewriter, making up stories. When doing neither, she can be found tending her overgrown garden (old-fashioned roses and irises are particular favourites). Her interest in the natural world, both flora and fauna, goes back to early childhood and she has been a member of the Worldwide Fund for Nature almost since its inception. Her interest in myths and legends is of equal long-standing.

TERRY MYLER trained at the National College of Art in Dublin, and also studied under her father, Seán O'Sullivan, RHA. She specialises in illustration and has done a lot of work for The Children's Press. Titles include *The Silent Sea, The Legend of the Golden Key, Cornelius Rabbit of Tang, Cornelius on Holidays, The Children of the Forge, Murtagh and the Vikings,* and *Save the Unicorns.*
She lives in the Wicklow hills, with her husband, two dogs and a cat. She has one daughter.

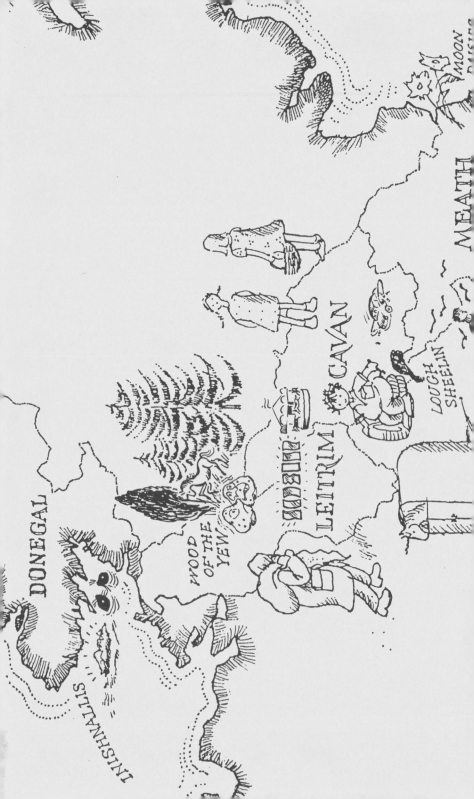